The Good Neighbors

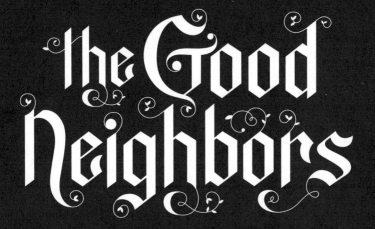

WHAT HAS COME BEFORE

When **Rue Silver** was a little girl, she saw daffodils bowing their flowered heads to her ethereal and strange mother, **Nia**. As she got older, Rue decided that even if she couldn't stop *being* crazy, she could stop *seeming* crazy like Nia. If Rue sees vines growing over buildings in a single night or people with animal faces, she simply ignores them.

When Rue's mother disappears after a loud argument with Rue's father, **Thaddeus**, Rue tries to ignore that, too. But then **Sarasa**, a girl at the university where Thaddeus teaches, is found dead. The police become convinced that Thaddeus murdered both his wife and Sarasa.

As Rue tries to figure out what actually happened, her grandfather, **Aubrey**, shows up. Not only does he seem not to have aged since her parents' wedding, but neither does his young servant, **Tam**. Rue comes to realize that Aubrey is one of the "good neighbors," faeries, and that he means to take over the city by encasing it in vines.

Rue also uncovers the fact that Thaddeus won Nia for his bride after passing a test. As with all faery bargains, there was a price: If Thaddeus was ever unfaithful, Nia would have to leave him. The night she disappeared, he'd had an affair with his friend **Amanda**.

Aubrey sends a changeling to pose as Nia. She is meant to sicken and die, so that no one will look for Nia anymore, but Rue sees through the trick. She and her friends dig up the body . . . and find a creature made of sticks.

Rue's mother has disappeared again. . . .

the Good neighbors

By
HOLLY BLACK
& TED NAIFEH

book two
KITH

graphix

New York   Toronto   London   Auckland   Sydney   Mexico City   New Delhi   Hong Kong

All rights reserved. Published by Graphix, an imprint of Scholastic Inc., Publishers since 1920. SCHOLASTIC, GRAPHIX, and associated logos are trademarks and/or registered trademarks of Scholastic Inc.

Library of Congress Cataloging-in-Publication Data Available

ISBN-13: 978-0-439-85563-1
ISBN-10: 0-439-85563-2

10 9 8 7 6 5 4 3 2 1   09 10 11 12 13

First edition, October 2009
"Good Neighbors" title lettering by Jessica Hische
Lettering by John Green
Edited by David Levithan
Book design by Phil Falco
Creative Director: David Saylor
Printed in the U.S.A.   23

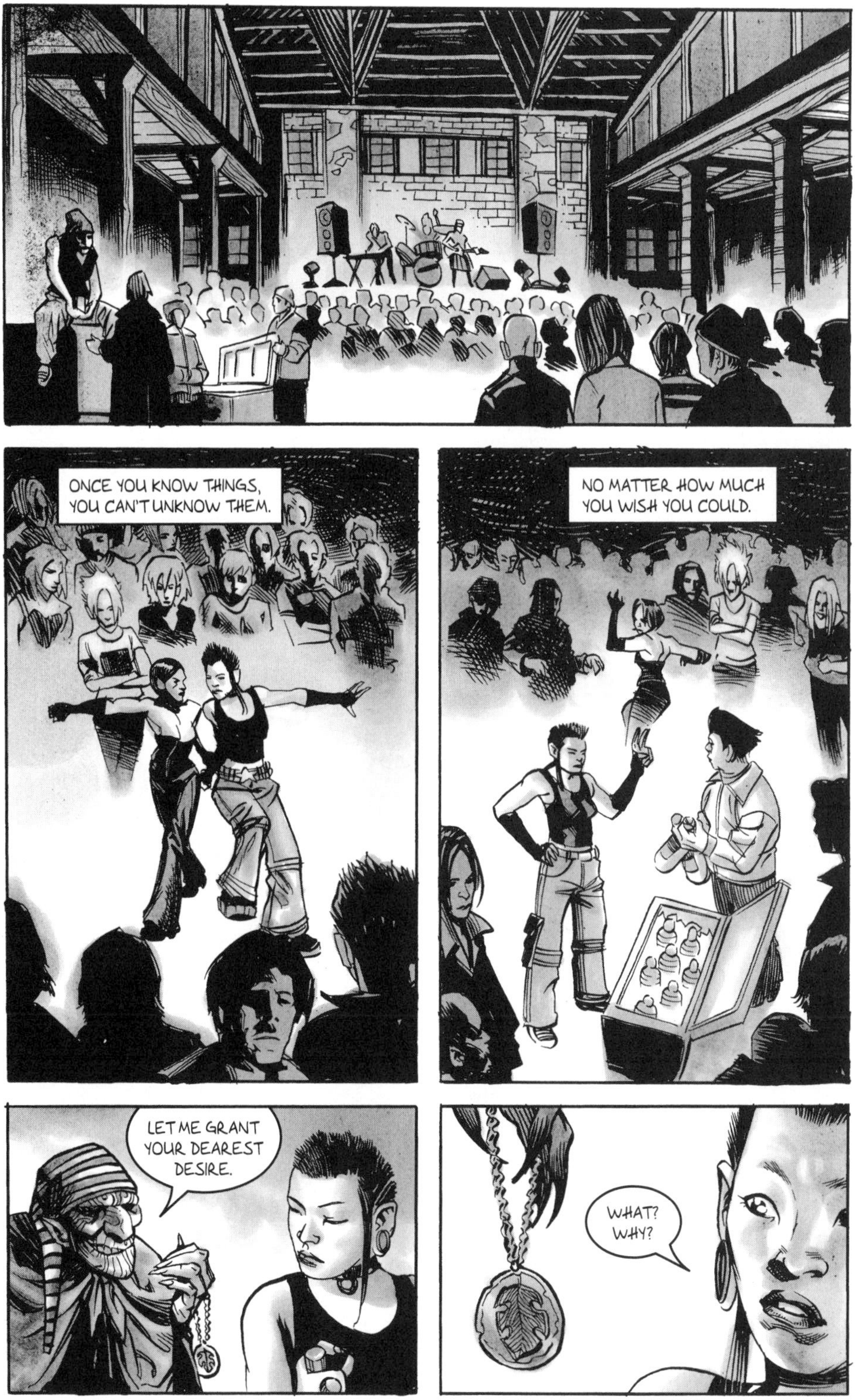
ONCE YOU KNOW THINGS, YOU CAN'T UNKNOW THEM.
NO MATTER HOW MUCH YOU WISH YOU COULD.
LET ME GRANT YOUR DEAREST DESIRE.
WHAT? WHY?

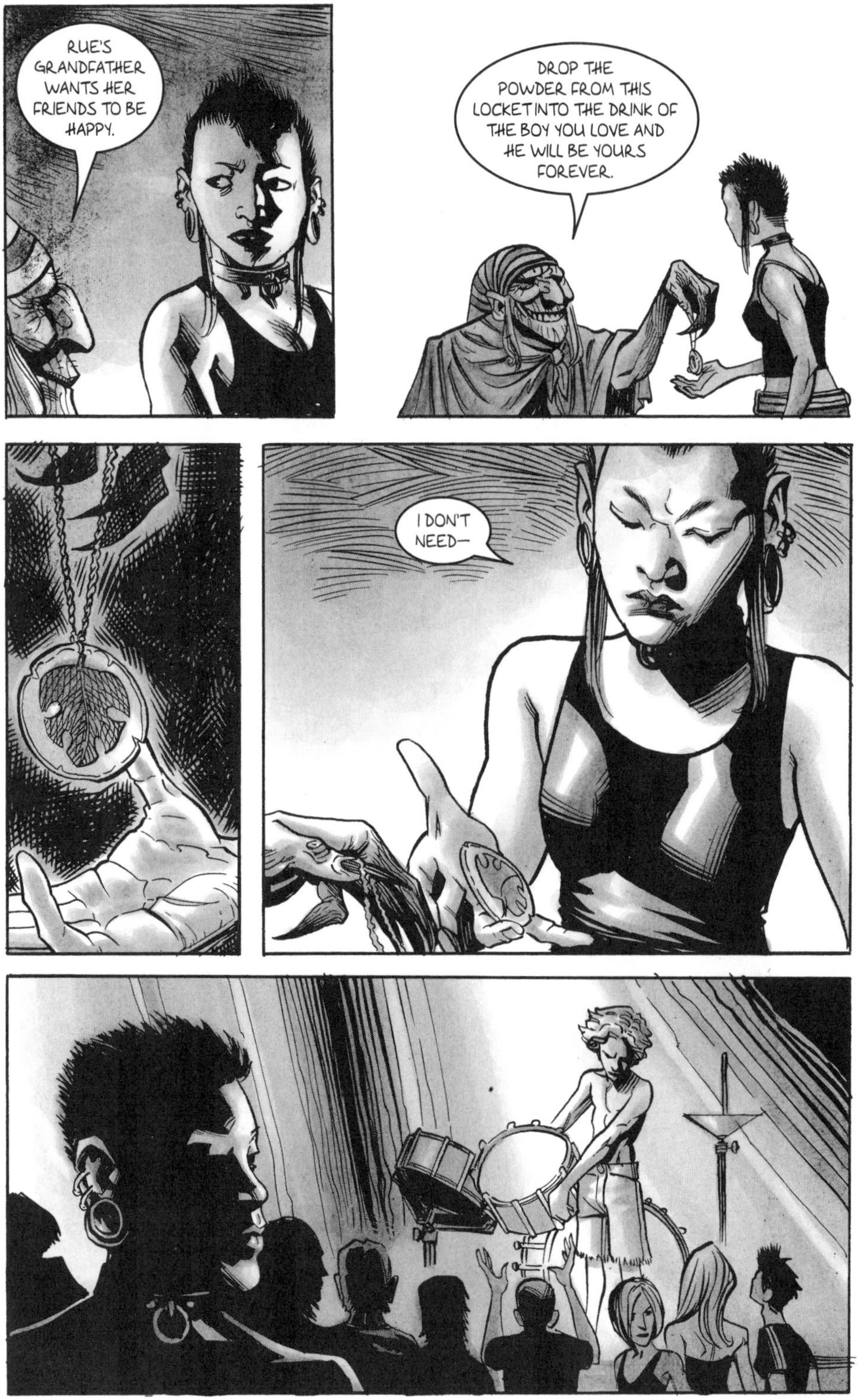
RUE'S GRANDFATHER WANTS HER FRIENDS TO BE HAPPY.
DROP THE POWDER FROM THIS LOCKET INTO THE DRINK OF THE BOY YOU LOVE AND HE WILL BE YOURS FOREVER.
I DON'T NEED—

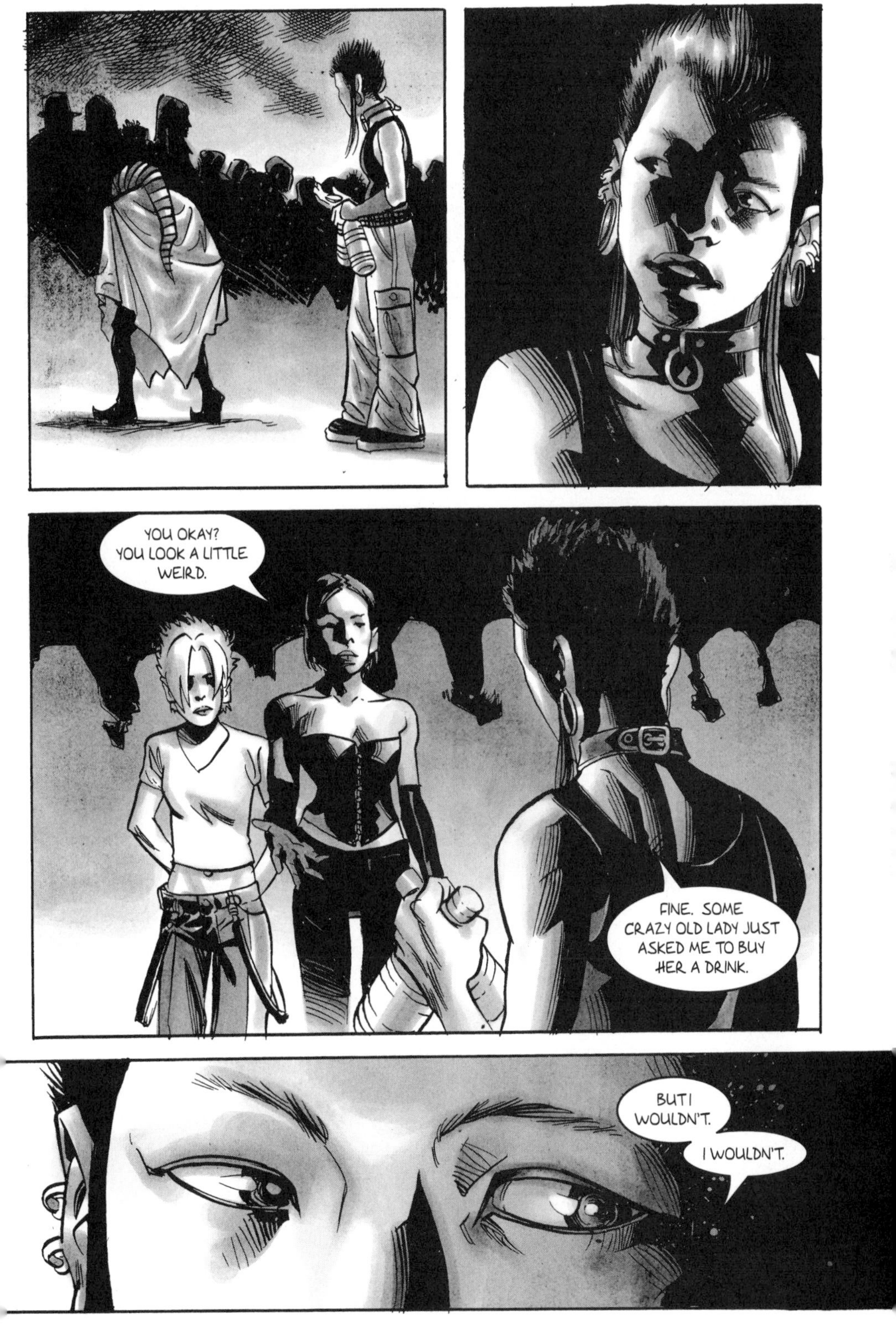
YOU OKAY? YOU LOOK A LITTLE WEIRD.
FINE. SOME CRAZY OLD LADY JUST ASKED ME TO BUY HER A DRINK.
BUT I WOULDN'T.
I WOULDN'T.

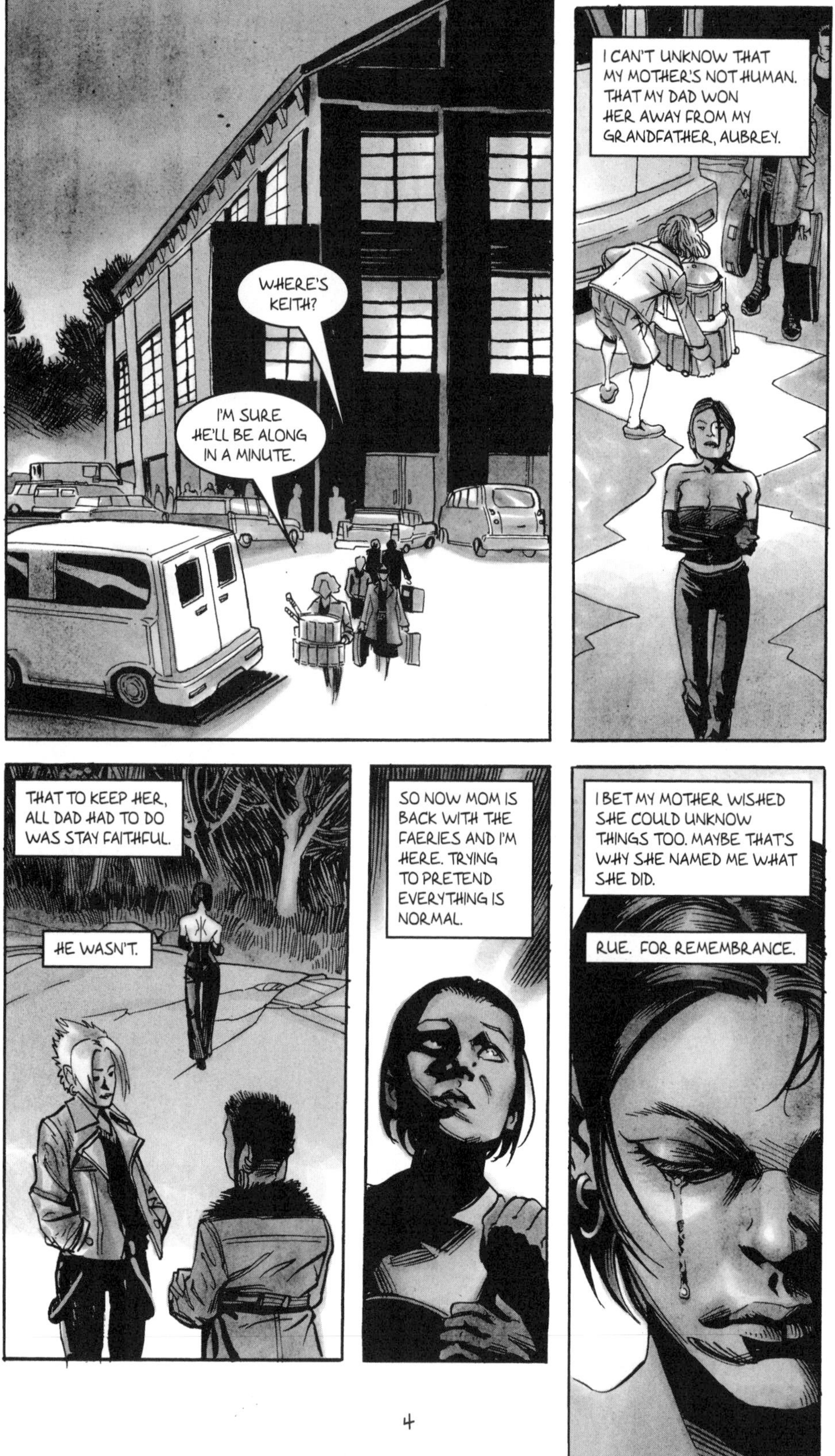
WHERE'S KEITH?
I'M SURE HE'LL BE ALONG IN A MINUTE.
I CAN'T UNKNOW THAT MY MOTHER'S NOT HUMAN. THAT MY DAD WON HER AWAY FROM MY GRANDFATHER, AUBREY.
THAT TO KEEP HER, ALL DAD HAD TO DO WAS STAY FAITHFUL.
HE WASN'T.
SO NOW MOM IS BACK WITH THE FAERIES AND I'M HERE. TRYING TO PRETEND EVERYTHING IS NORMAL.
I BET MY MOTHER WISHED SHE COULD UNKNOW THINGS TOO. MAYBE THAT'S WHY SHE NAMED ME WHAT SHE DID.
RUE. FOR REMEMBRANCE.

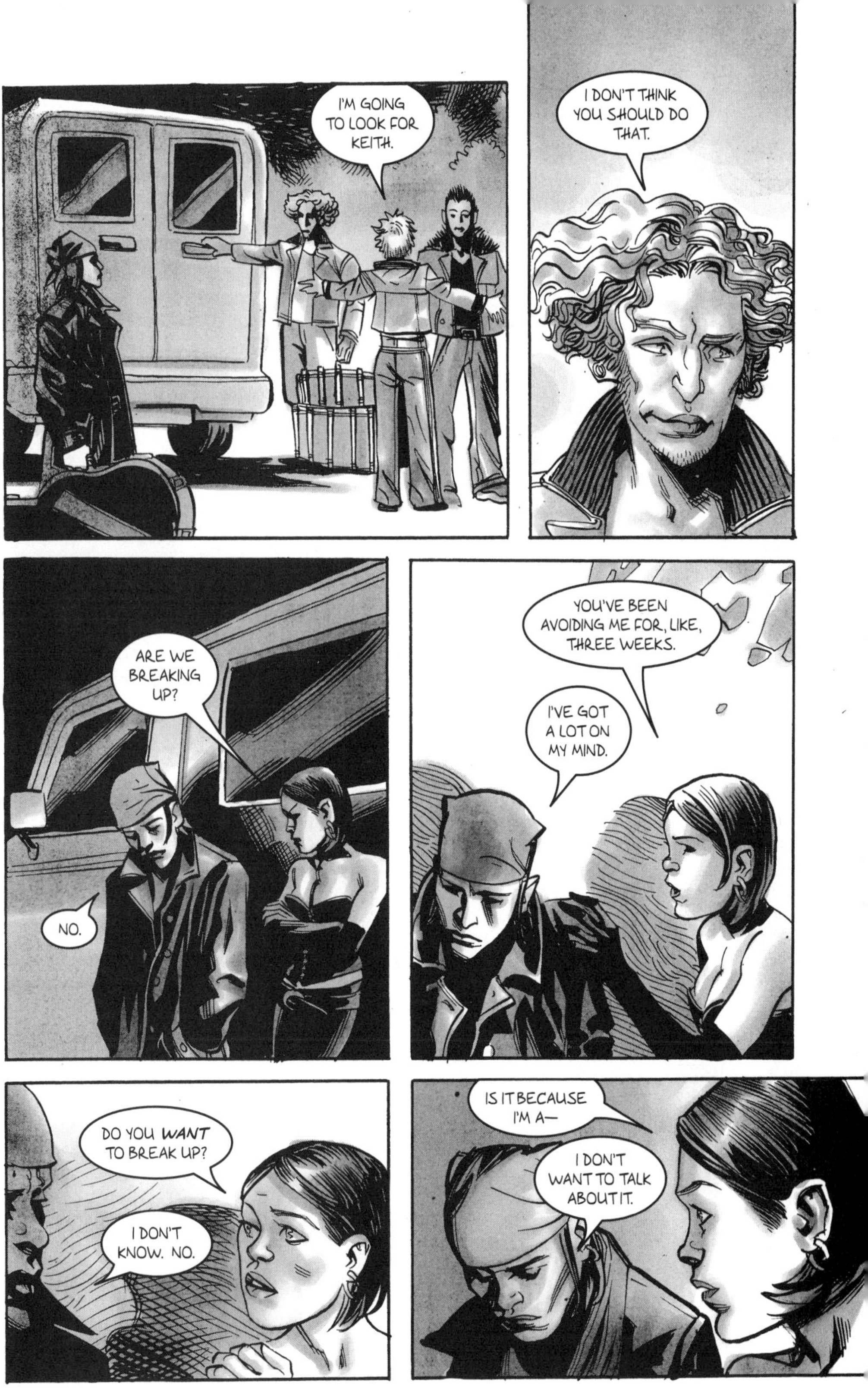
I'M GOING TO LOOK FOR KEITH.
I DON'T THINK YOU SHOULD DO THAT.
ARE WE BREAKING UP?
NO.
YOU'VE BEEN AVOIDING ME FOR, LIKE, THREE WEEKS.
I'VE GOT A LOT ON MY MIND.
DO YOU *WANT* TO BREAK UP?
I DON'T KNOW. NO.
IS IT BECAUSE I'M A—
I DON'T WANT TO TALK ABOUT IT.

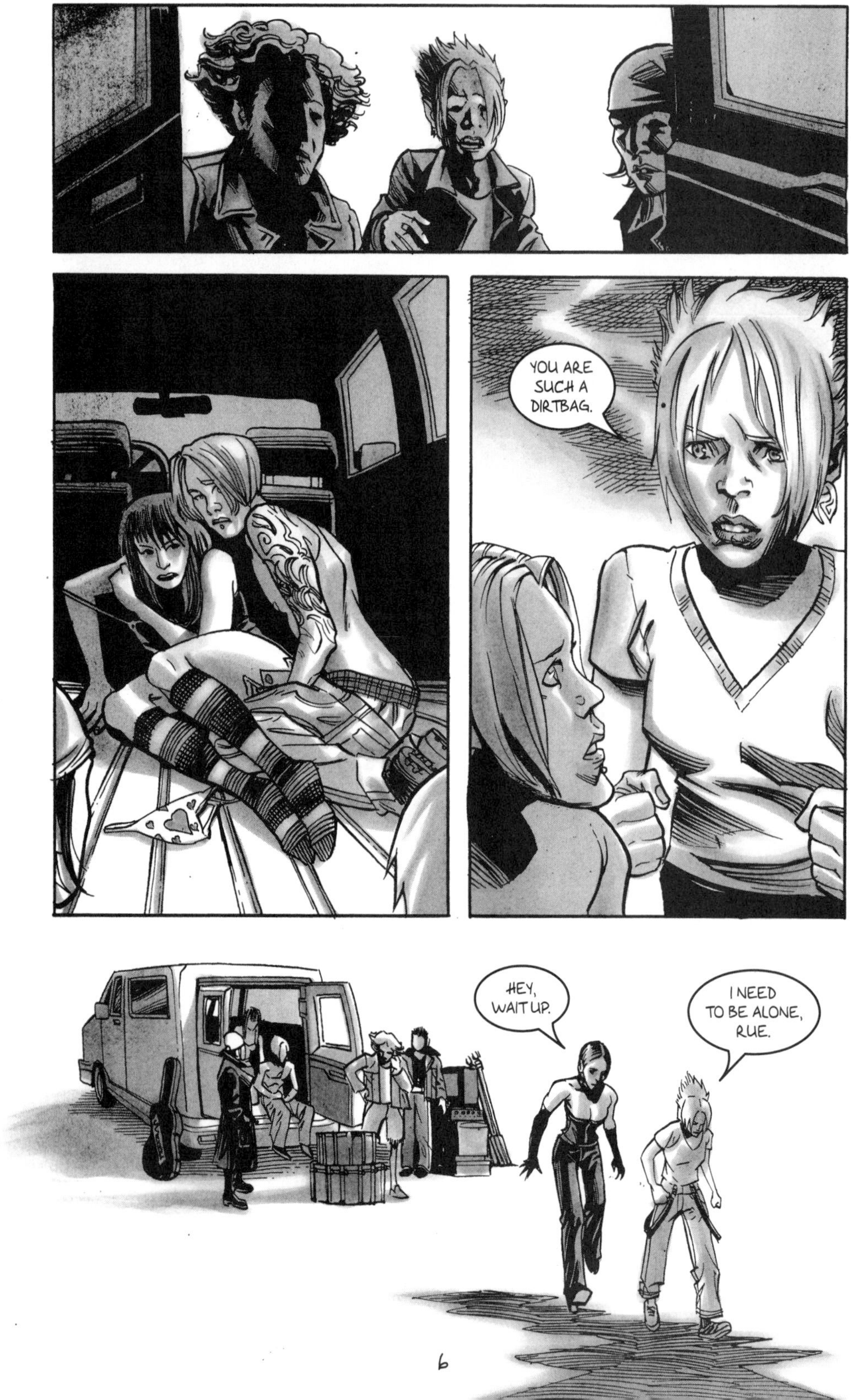
YOU ARE SUCH A DIRTBAG.
HEY, WAIT UP.
I NEED TO BE ALONE, RUE.

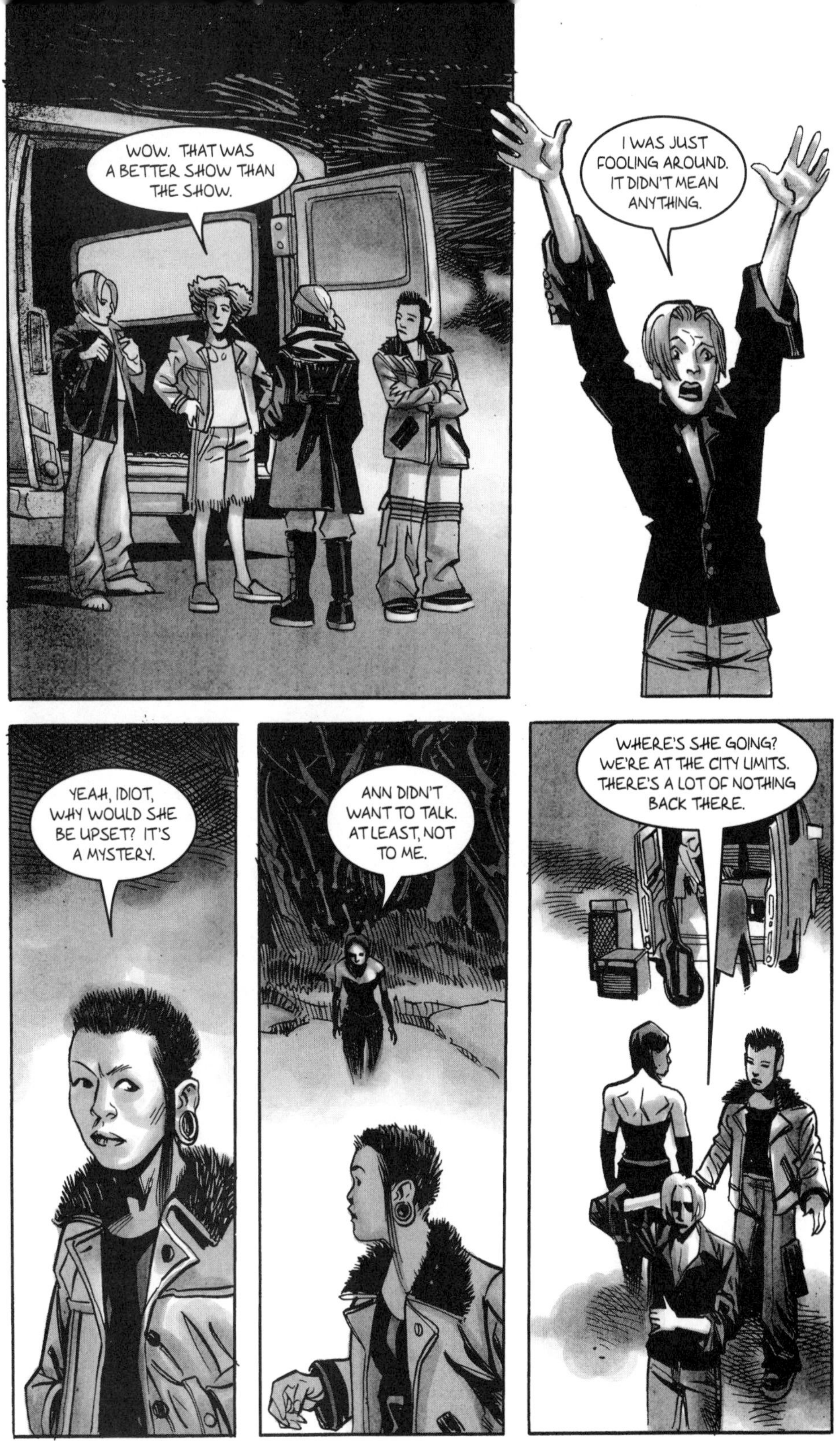
WOW. THAT WAS A BETTER SHOW THAN THE SHOW.
I WAS JUST FOOLING AROUND. IT DIDN'T MEAN ANYTHING.
YEAH, IDIOT, WHY WOULD SHE BE UPSET? IT'S A MYSTERY.
ANN DIDN'T WANT TO TALK. AT LEAST, NOT TO ME.
WHERE'S SHE GOING? WE'RE AT THE CITY LIMITS. THERE'S A LOT OF NOTHING BACK THERE.

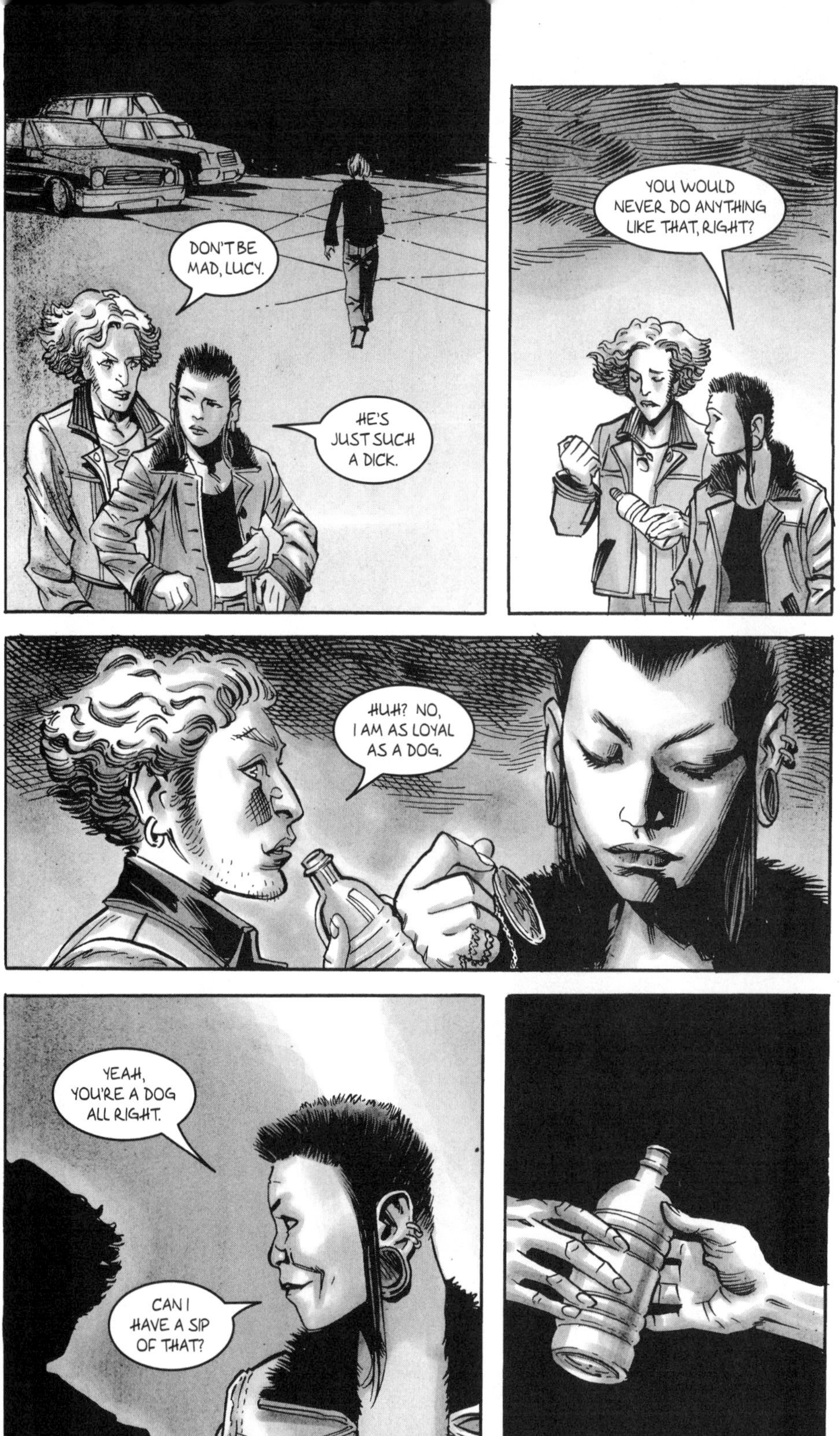
DON'T BE MAD, LUCY.
HE'S JUST SUCH A DICK.
YOU WOULD NEVER DO ANYTHING LIKE THAT, RIGHT?
HUH? NO, I AM AS LOYAL AS A DOG.
YEAH, YOU'RE A DOG ALL RIGHT.
CAN I HAVE A SIP OF THAT?

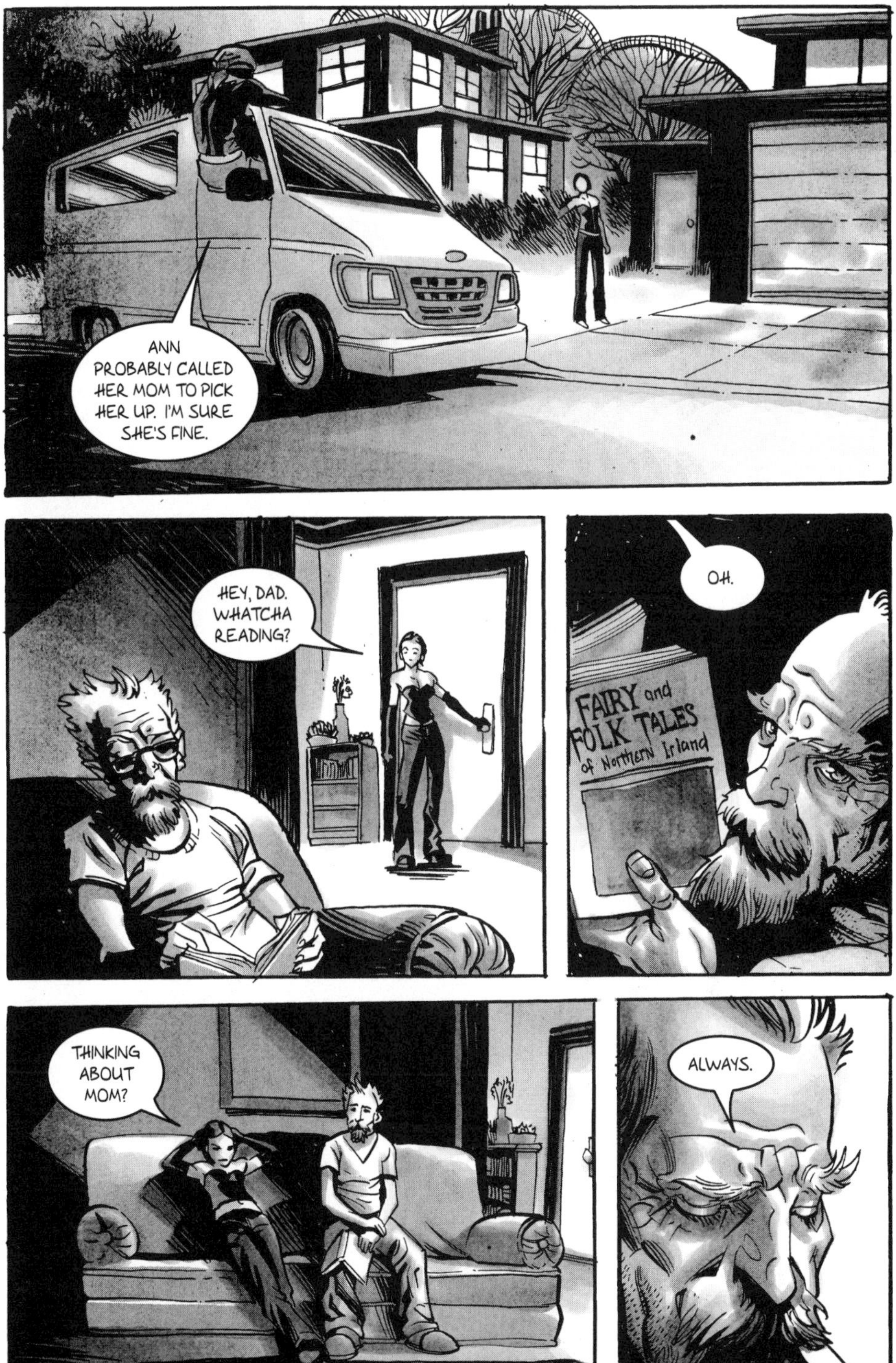
ANN PROBABLY CALLED HER MOM TO PICK HER UP. I'M SURE SHE'S FINE.
HEY, DAD. WHATCHA READING?
OH.
FAIRY and FOLK TALES of Northern Irland
THINKING ABOUT MOM?
ALWAYS.

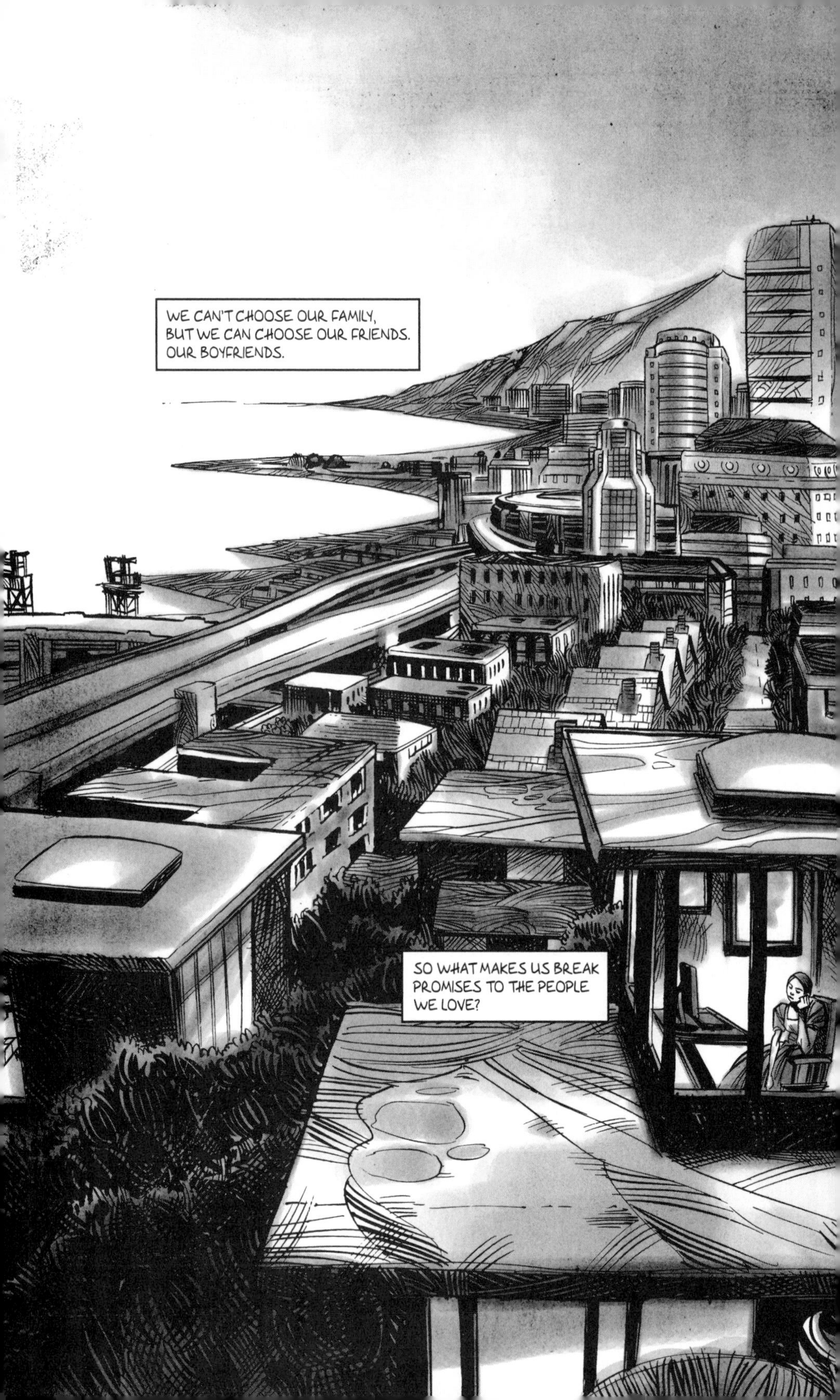
WE CAN'T CHOOSE OUR FAMILY, BUT WE CAN CHOOSE OUR FRIENDS. OUR BOYFRIENDS.
SO WHAT MAKES US BREAK PROMISES TO THE PEOPLE WE LOVE?

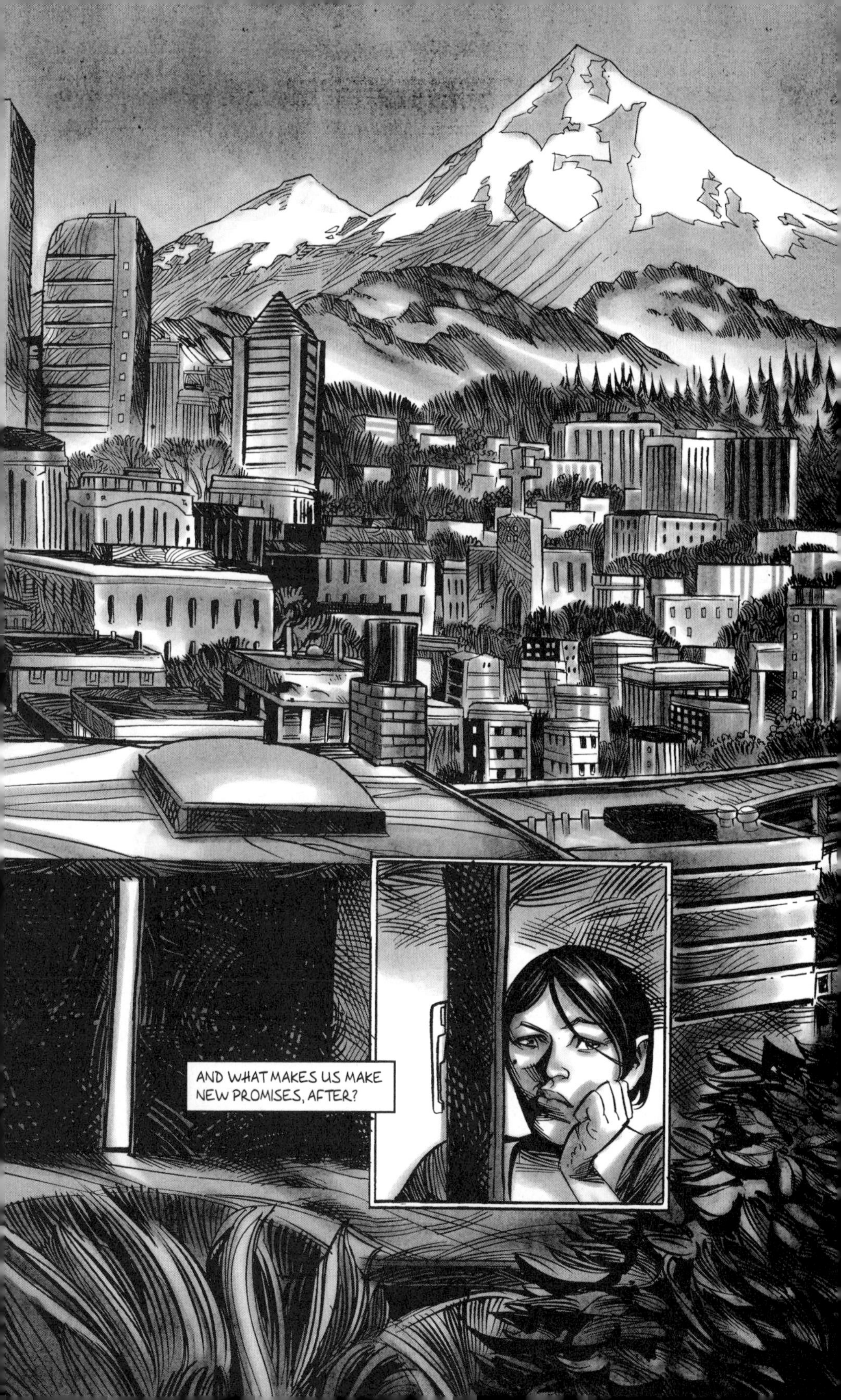
AND WHAT MAKES US MAKE
NEW PROMISES, AFTER?

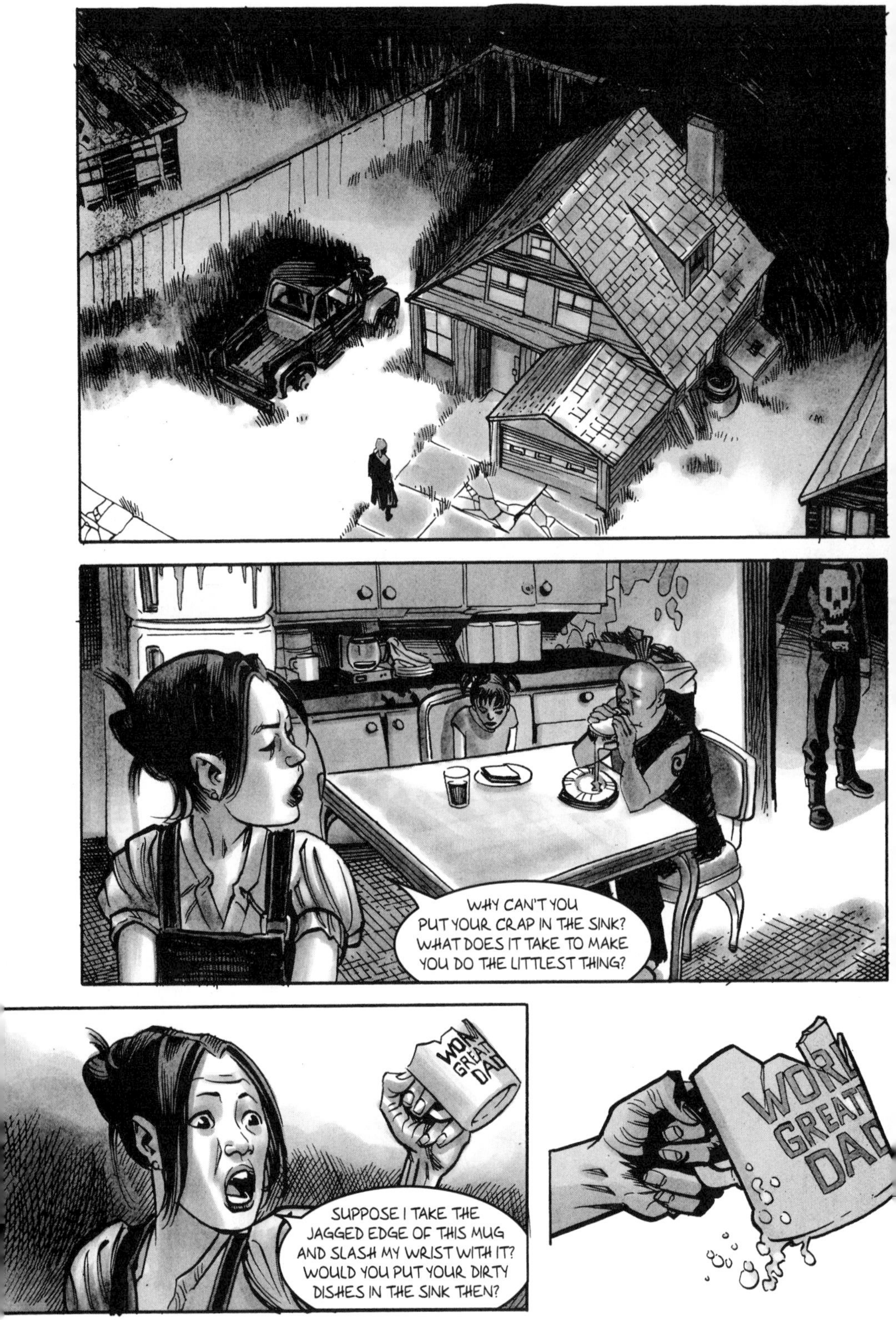
WHY CAN'T YOU PUT YOUR CRAP IN THE SINK? WHAT DOES IT TAKE TO MAKE YOU DO THE LITTLEST THING?
WOR GREAT DAD
SUPPOSE I TAKE THE JAGGED EDGE OF THIS MUG AND SLASH MY WRIST WITH IT? WOULD YOU PUT YOUR DIRTY DISHES IN THE SINK THEN?
WOR GREAT DAD

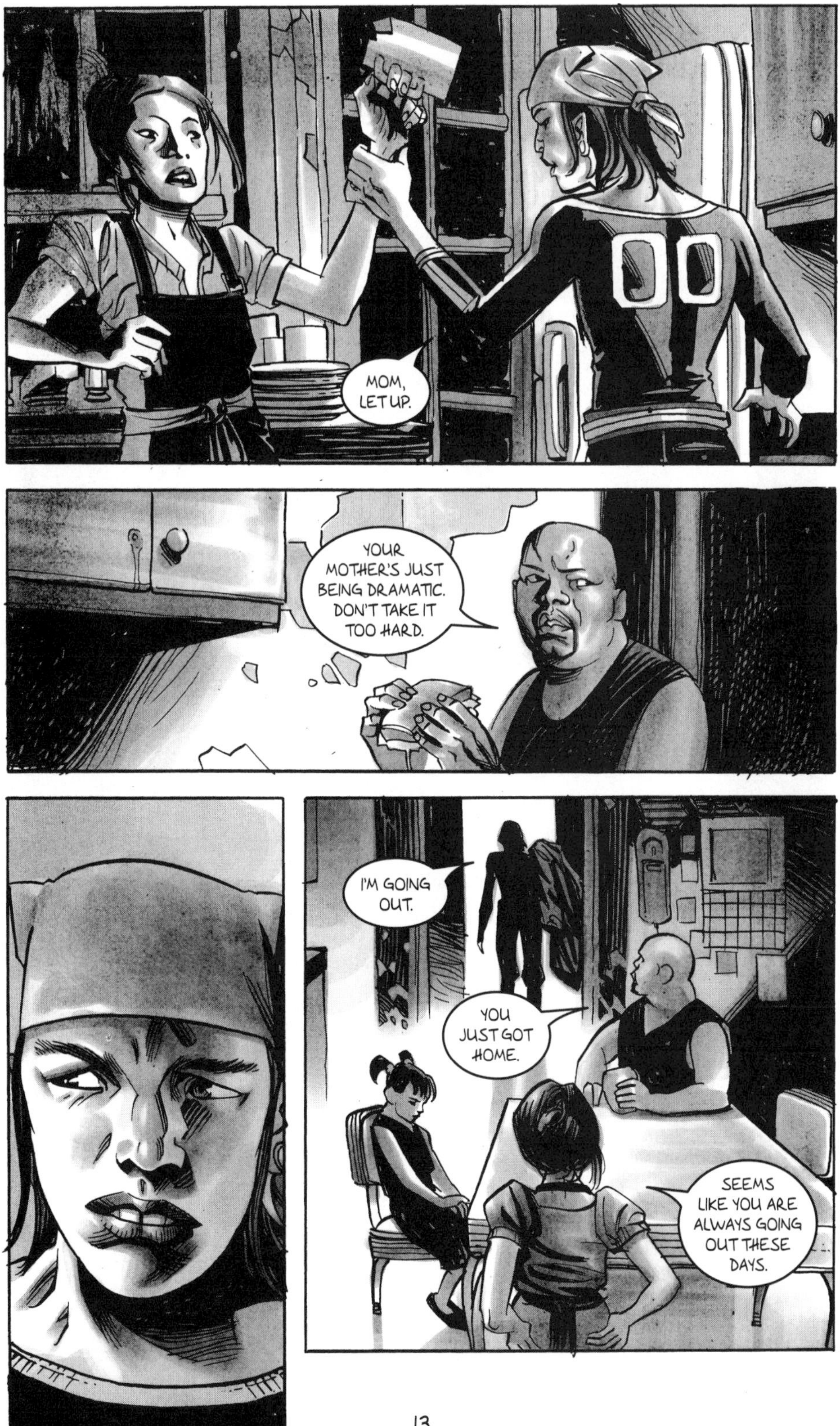
MOM, LET UP.
YOUR MOTHER'S JUST BEING DRAMATIC. DON'T TAKE IT TOO HARD.
I'M GOING OUT.
YOU JUST GOT HOME.
SEEMS LIKE YOU ARE ALWAYS GOING OUT THESE DAYS.

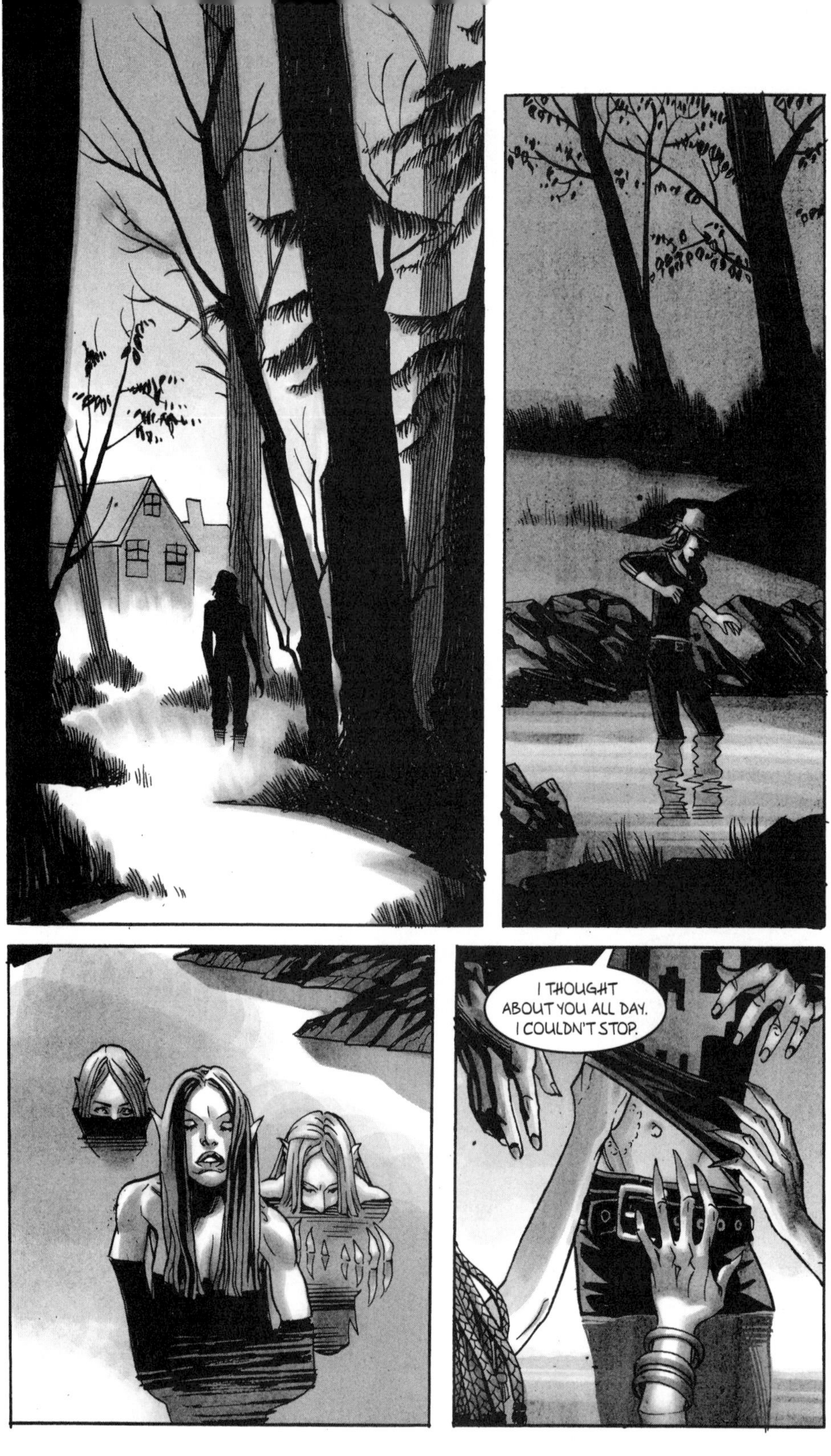
I THOUGHT ABOUT YOU ALL DAY. I COULDN'T STOP.

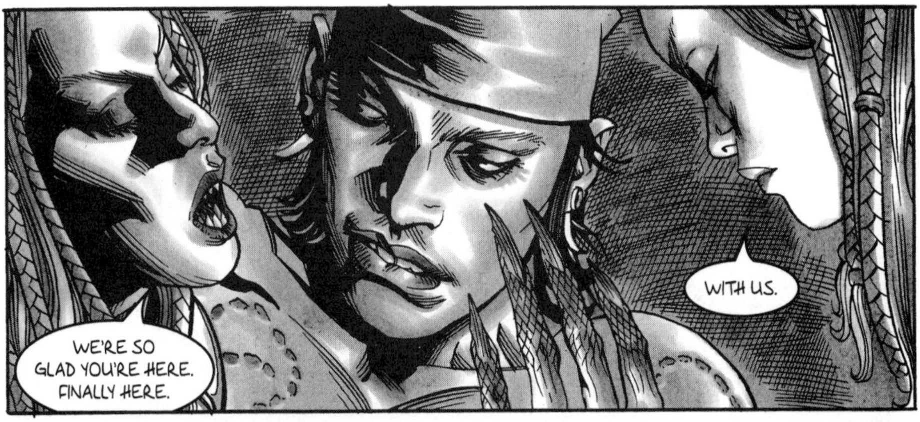
WE'RE SO GLAD YOU'RE HERE. FINALLY HERE.
WITH US.

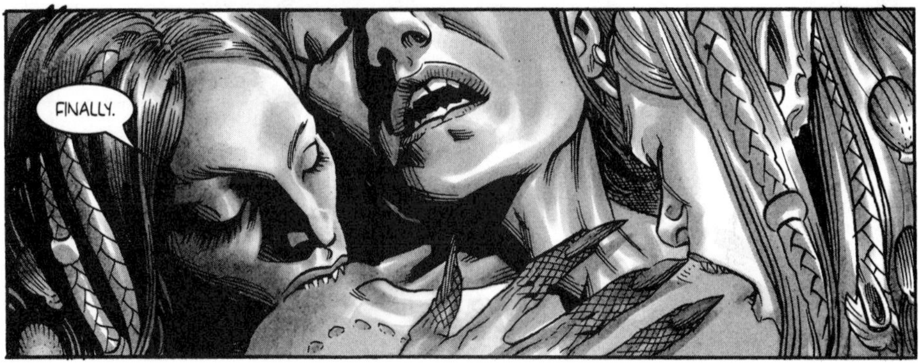
FINALLY.

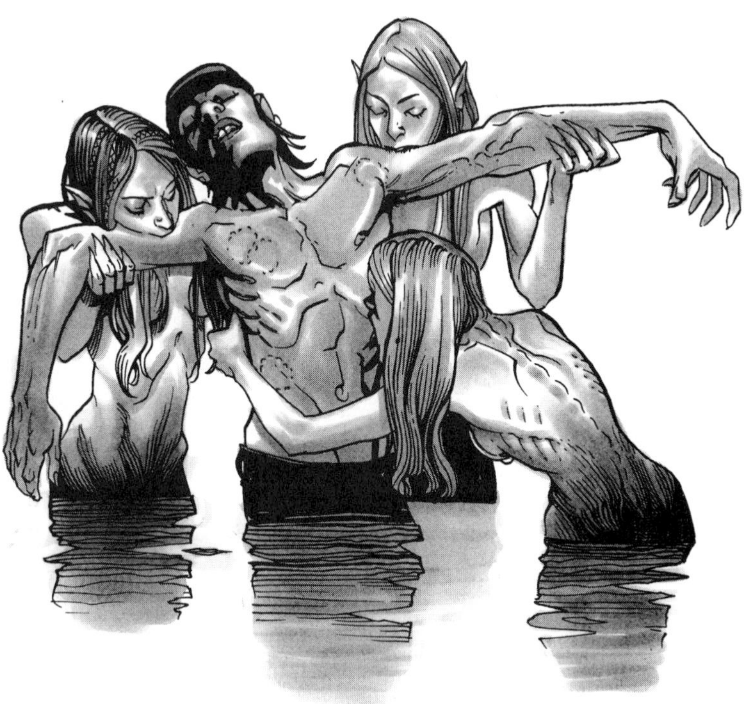

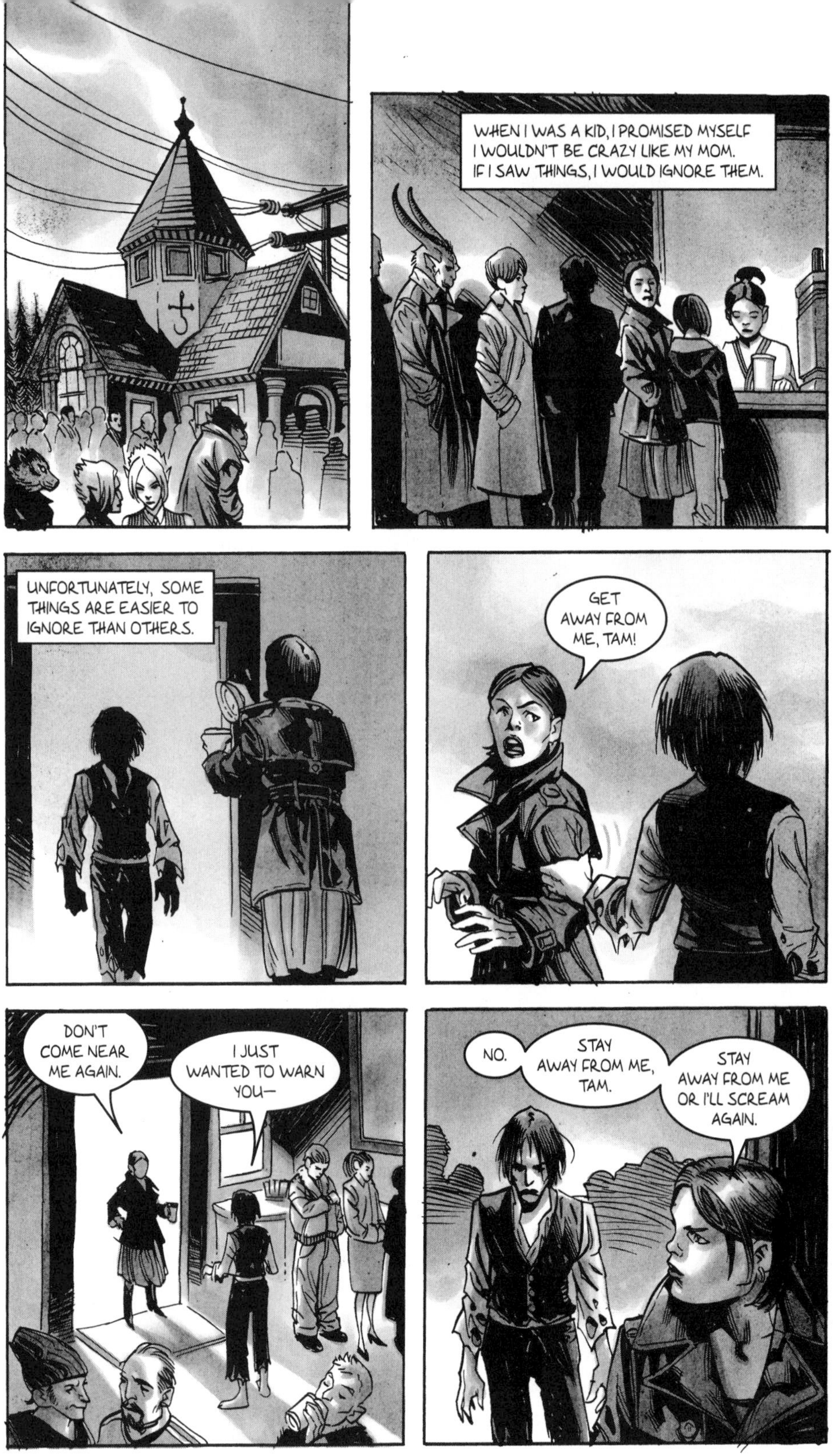

WHEN I WAS A KID, I PROMISED MYSELF I WOULDN'T BE CRAZY LIKE MY MOM. IF I SAW THINGS, I WOULD IGNORE THEM.
UNFORTUNATELY, SOME THINGS ARE EASIER TO IGNORE THAN OTHERS.
GET AWAY FROM ME, TAM!
DON'T COME NEAR ME AGAIN.
I JUST WANTED TO WARN YOU—
NO.
STAY AWAY FROM ME, TAM.
STAY AWAY FROM ME OR I'LL SCREAM AGAIN.

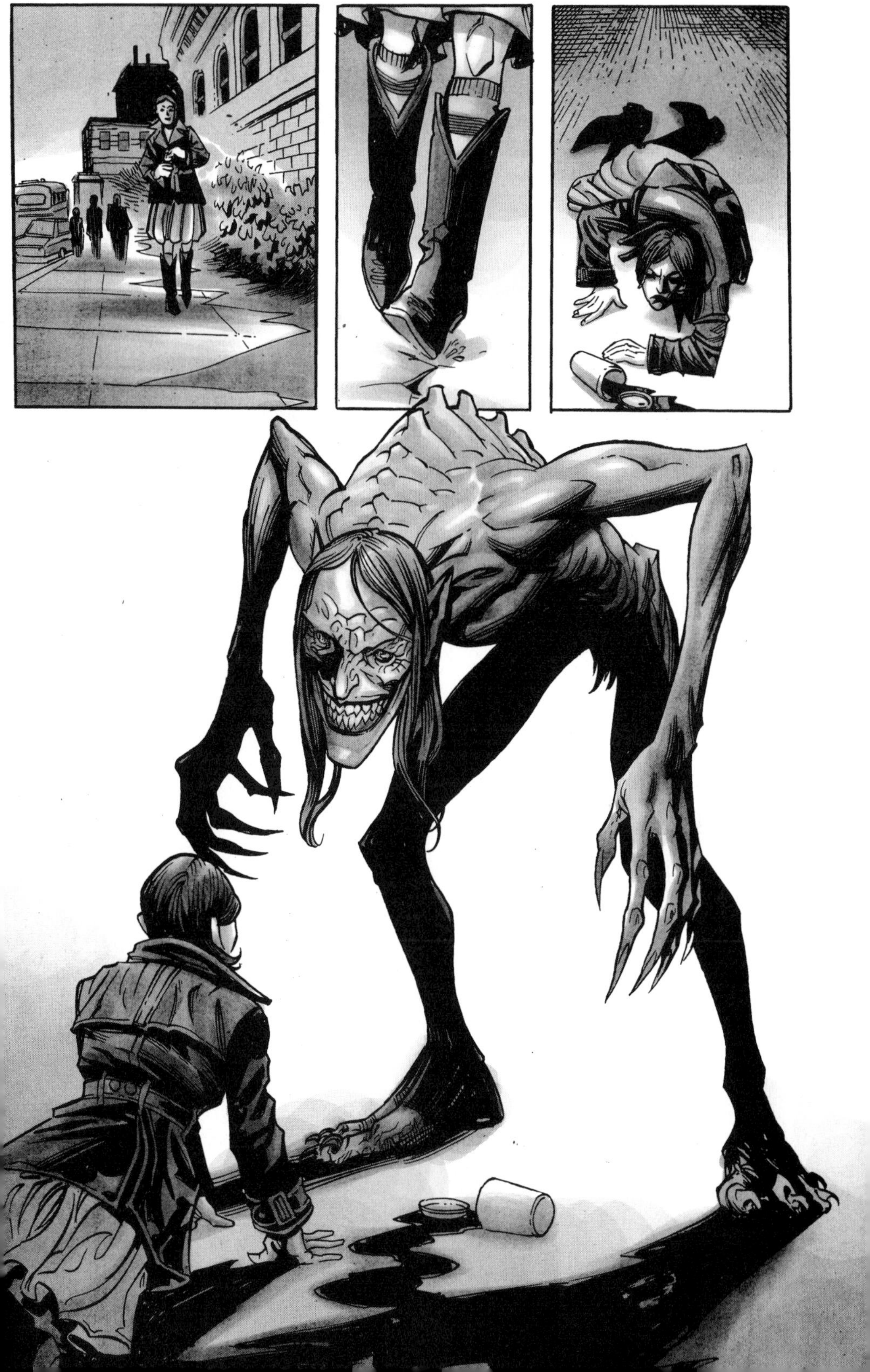

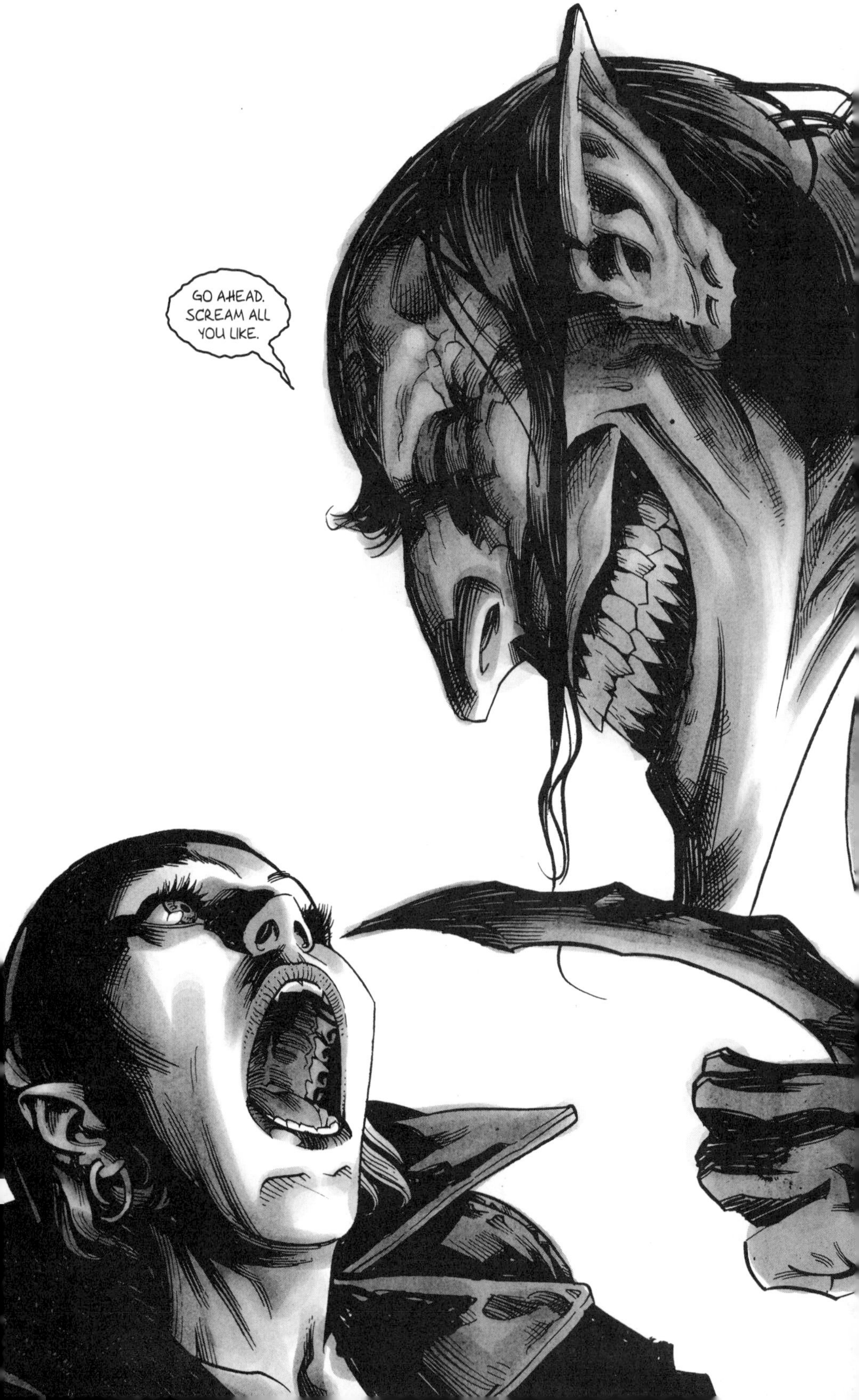
GO AHEAD. SCREAM ALL YOU LIKE.

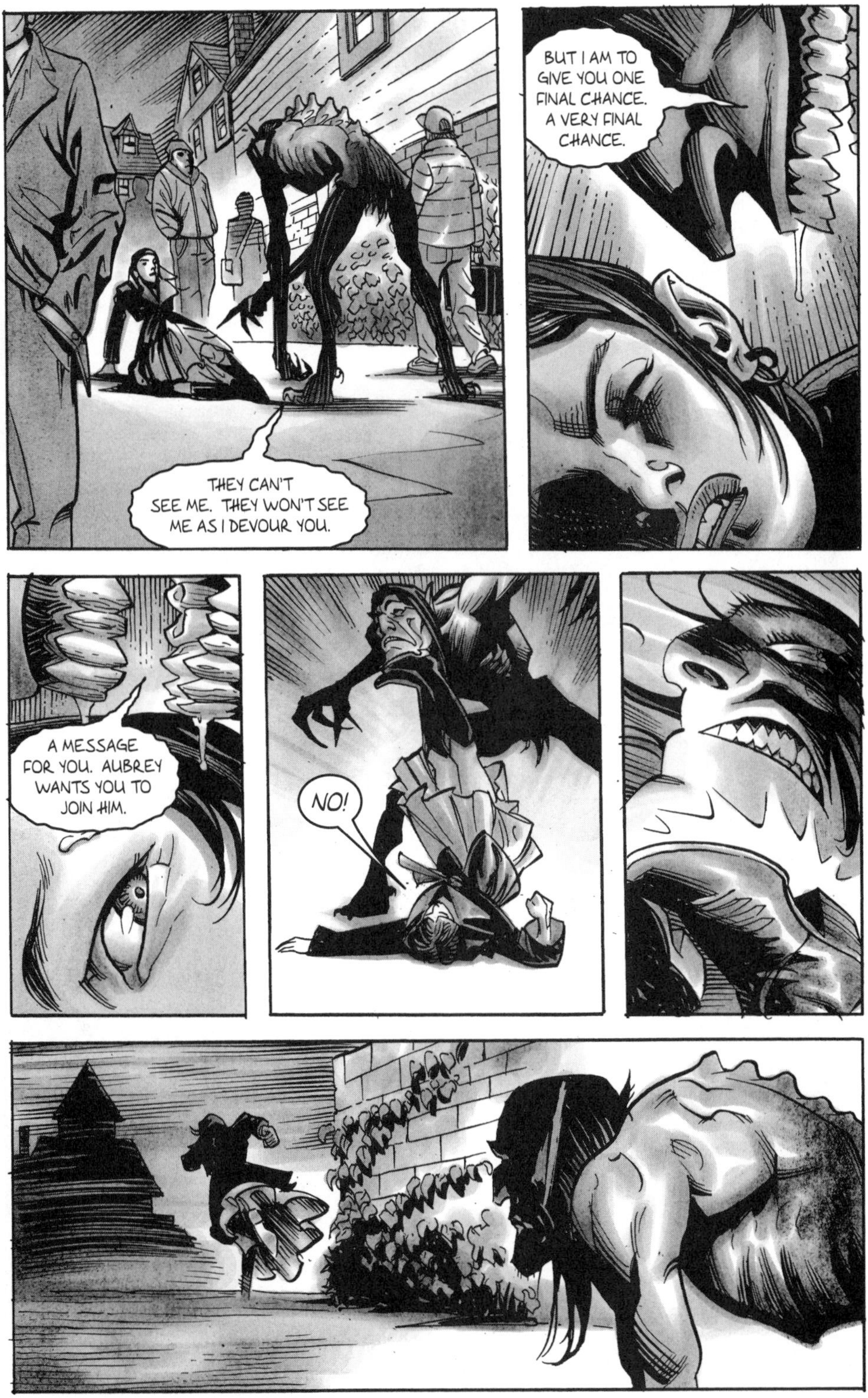
THEY CAN'T SEE ME. THEY WON'T SEE ME AS I DEVOUR YOU.
BUT I AM TO GIVE YOU ONE FINAL CHANCE. A VERY FINAL CHANCE.
A MESSAGE FOR YOU. AUBREY WANTS YOU TO JOIN HIM.
NO!

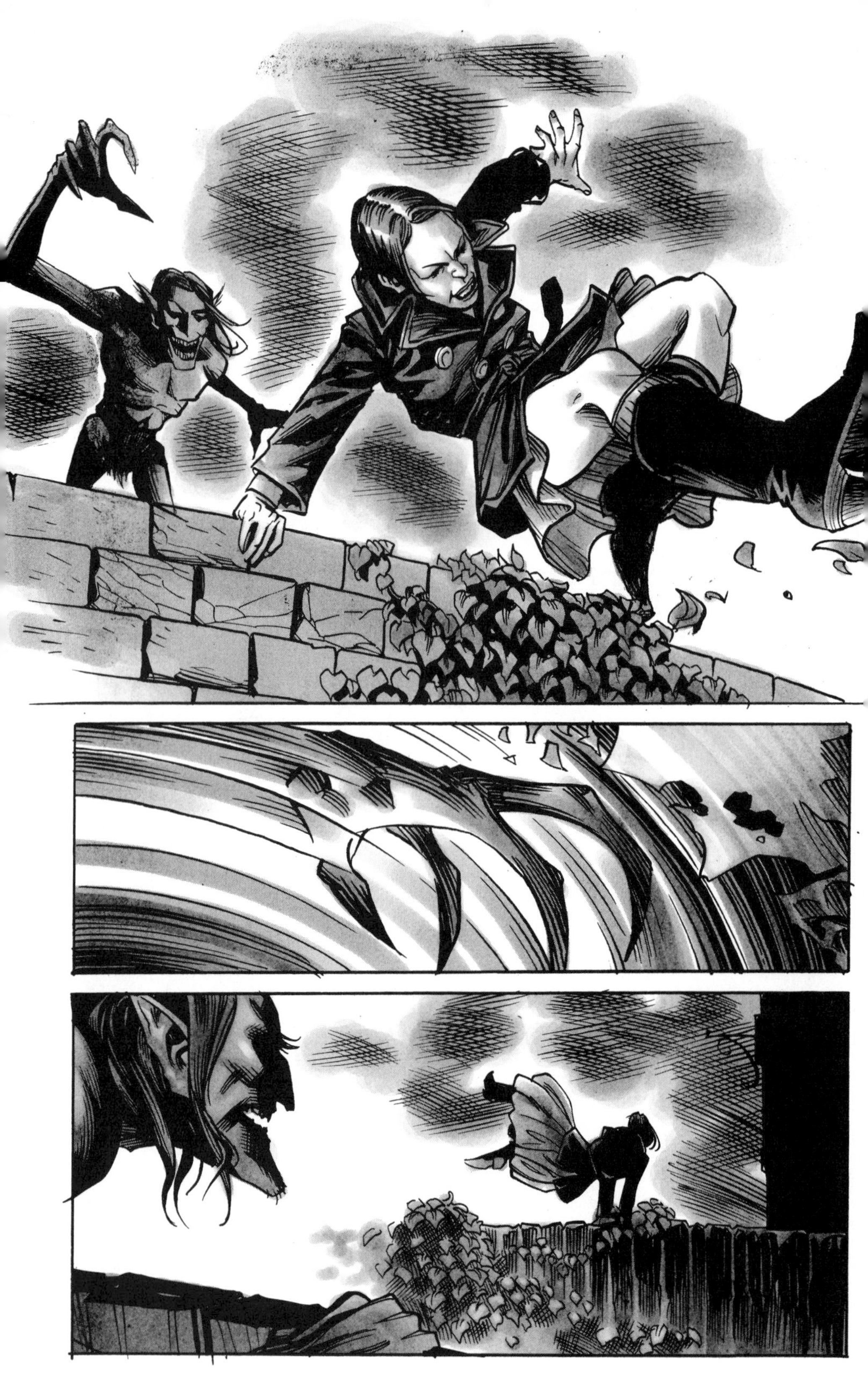

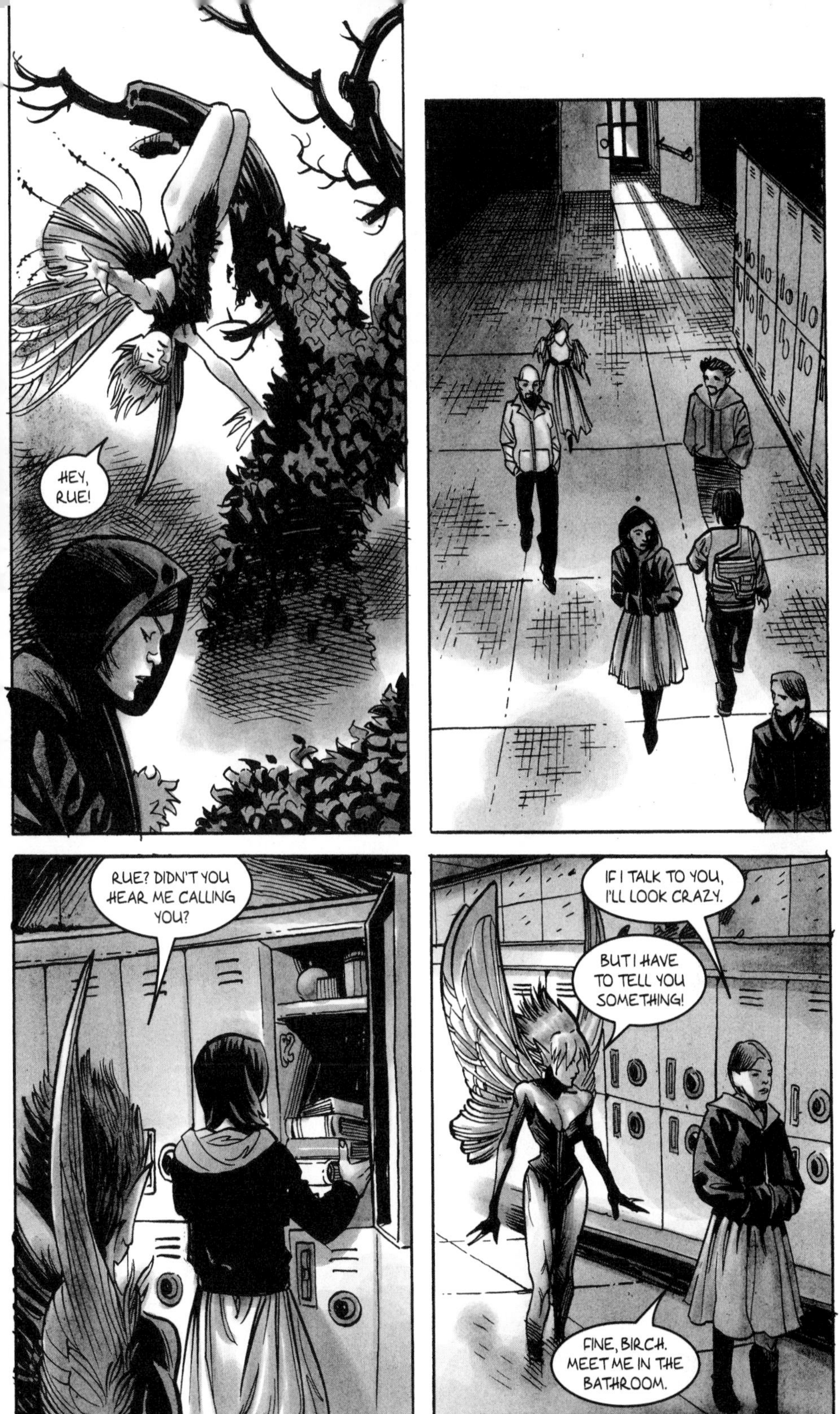

HEY, RUE!
RUE? DIDN'T YOU HEAR ME CALLING YOU?
IF I TALK TO YOU, I'LL LOOK CRAZY.
BUT I HAVE TO TELL YOU SOMETHING!
FINE, BIRCH. MEET ME IN THE BATHROOM.

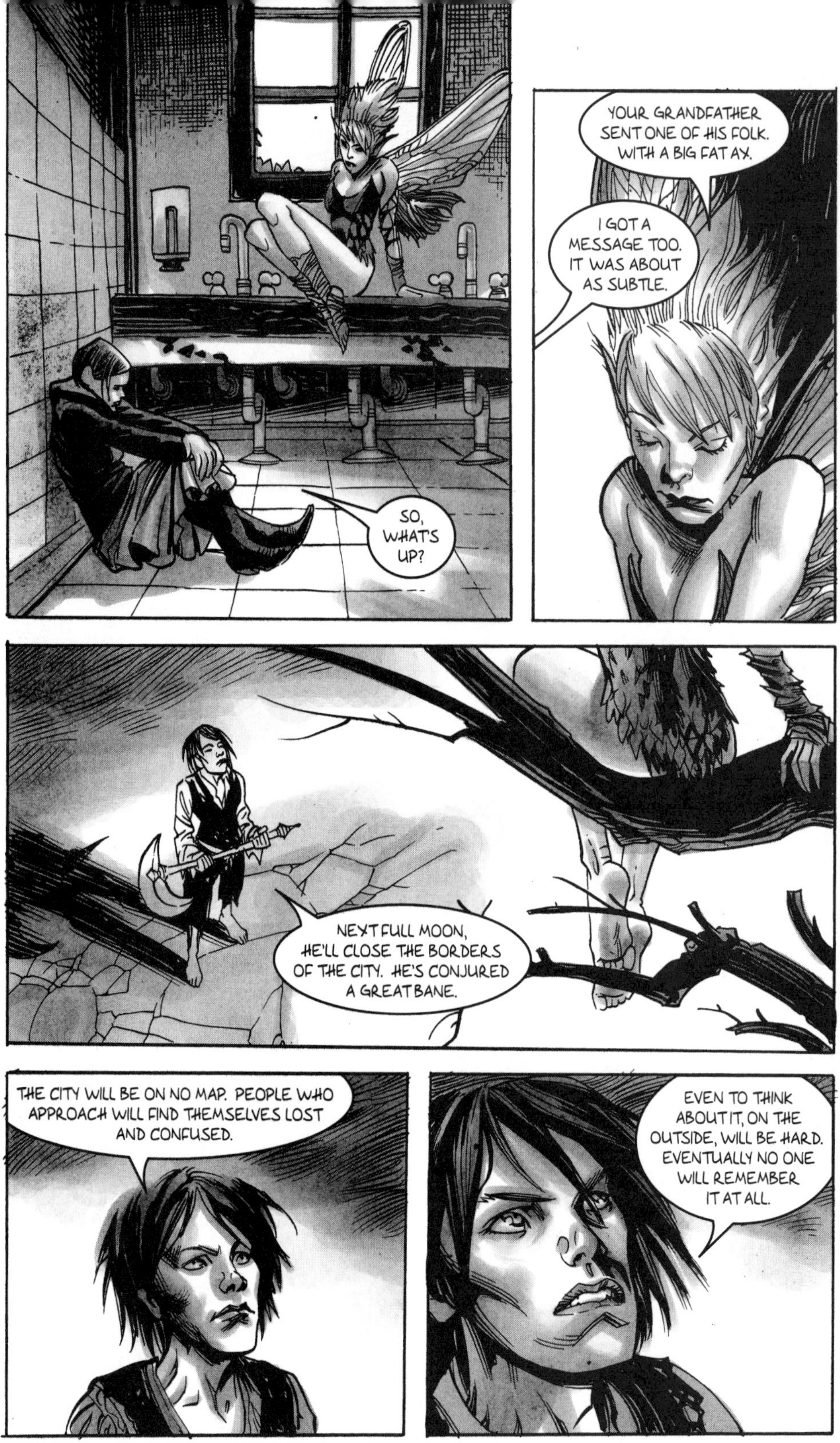
SO, WHAT'S UP?
YOUR GRANDFATHER SENT ONE OF HIS FOLK. WITH A BIG FAT AX.
I GOT A MESSAGE TOO. IT WAS ABOUT AS SUBTLE.
NEXT FULL MOON, HE'LL CLOSE THE BORDERS OF THE CITY. HE'S CONJURED A GREATBANE.
THE CITY WILL BE ON NO MAP. PEOPLE WHO APPROACH WILL FIND THEMSELVES LOST AND CONFUSED.
EVEN TO THINK ABOUT IT, ON THE OUTSIDE, WILL BE HARD. EVENTUALLY NO ONE WILL REMEMBER IT AT ALL.

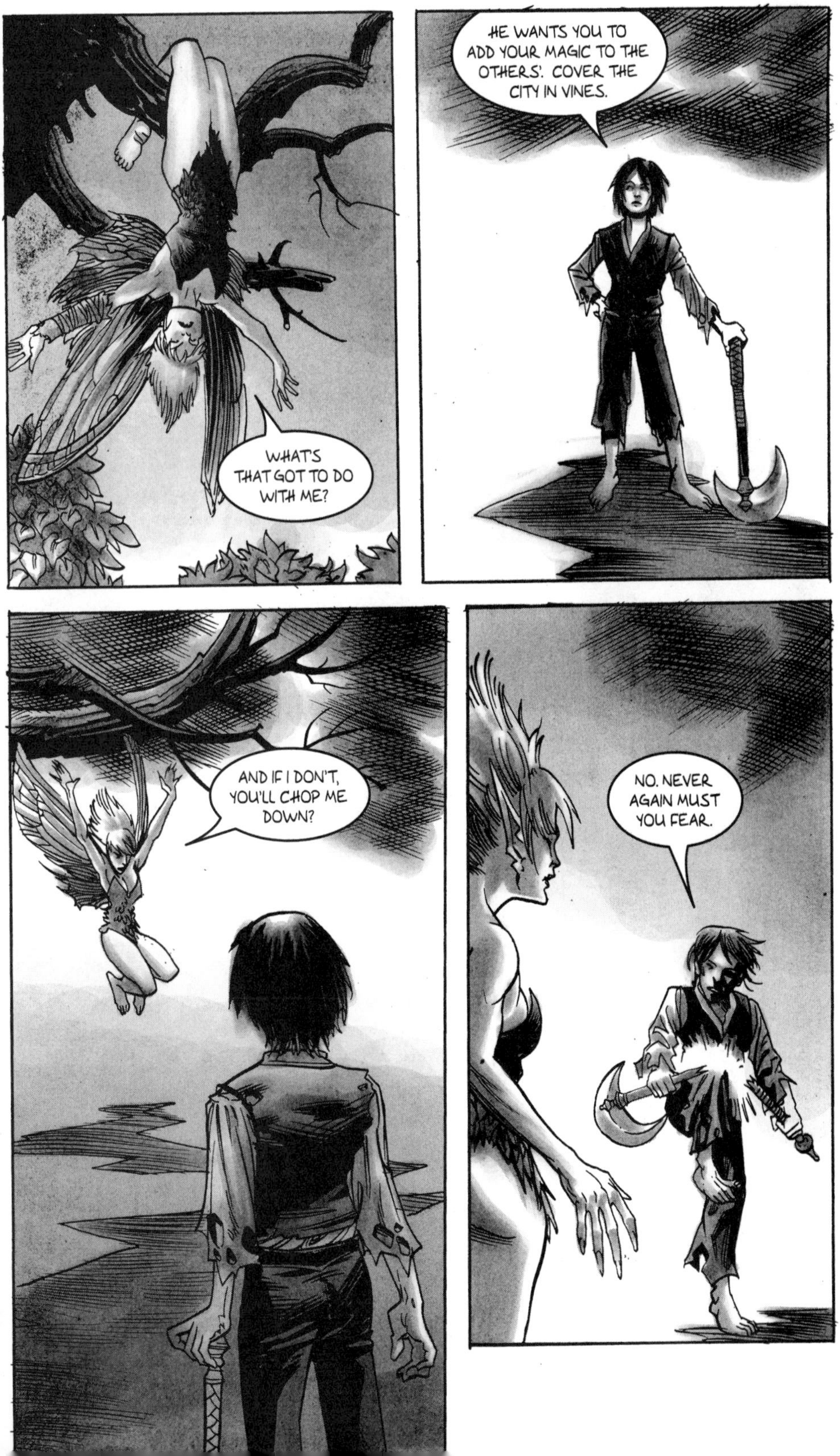
WHAT'S THAT GOT TO DO WITH ME?
HE WANTS YOU TO ADD YOUR MAGIC TO THE OTHERS'. COVER THE CITY IN VINES.
AND IF I DON'T, YOU'LL CHOP ME DOWN?
NO. NEVER AGAIN MUST YOU FEAR.

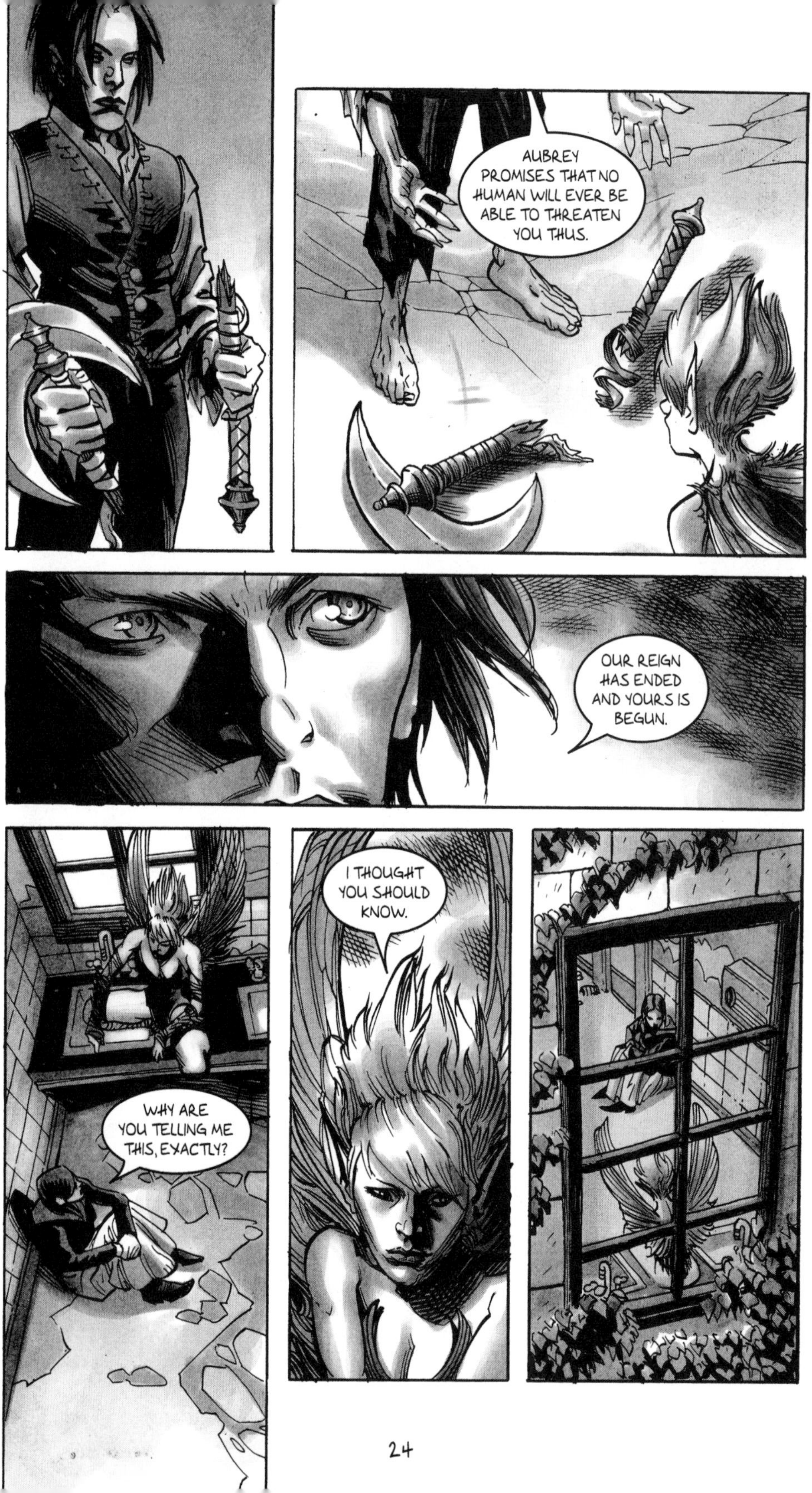
AUBREY PROMISES THAT NO HUMAN WILL EVER BE ABLE TO THREATEN YOU THUS.
OUR REIGN HAS ENDED AND YOURS IS BEGUN.
WHY ARE YOU TELLING ME THIS, EXACTLY?
I THOUGHT YOU SHOULD KNOW.

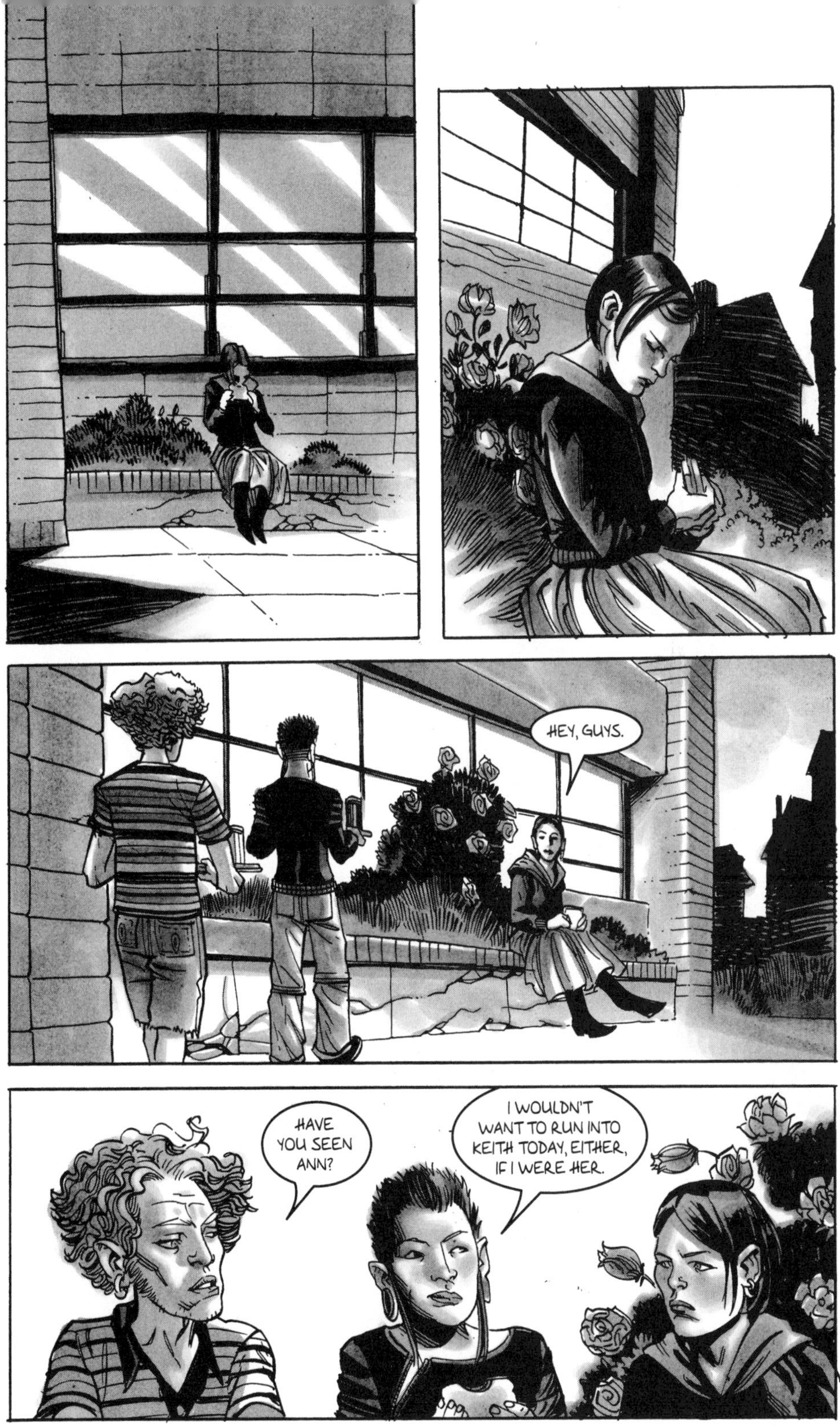
HEY, GUYS.
HAVE YOU SEEN ANN?
I WOULDN'T WANT TO RUN INTO KEITH TODAY, EITHER, IF I WERE HER.

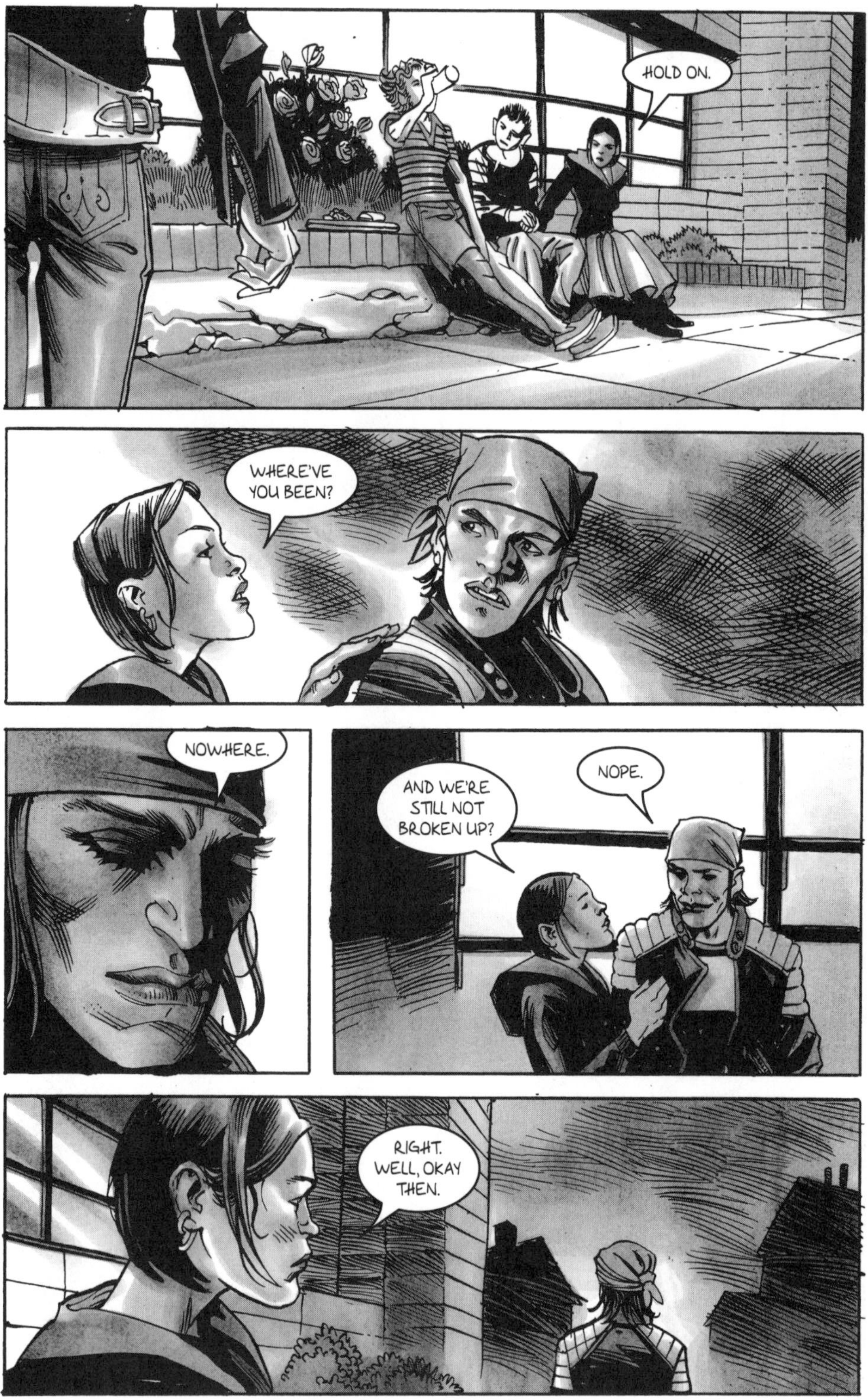
HOLD ON.
WHERE'VE YOU BEEN?
NOWHERE.
AND WE'RE STILL NOT BROKEN UP?
NOPE.
RIGHT. WELL, OKAY THEN.

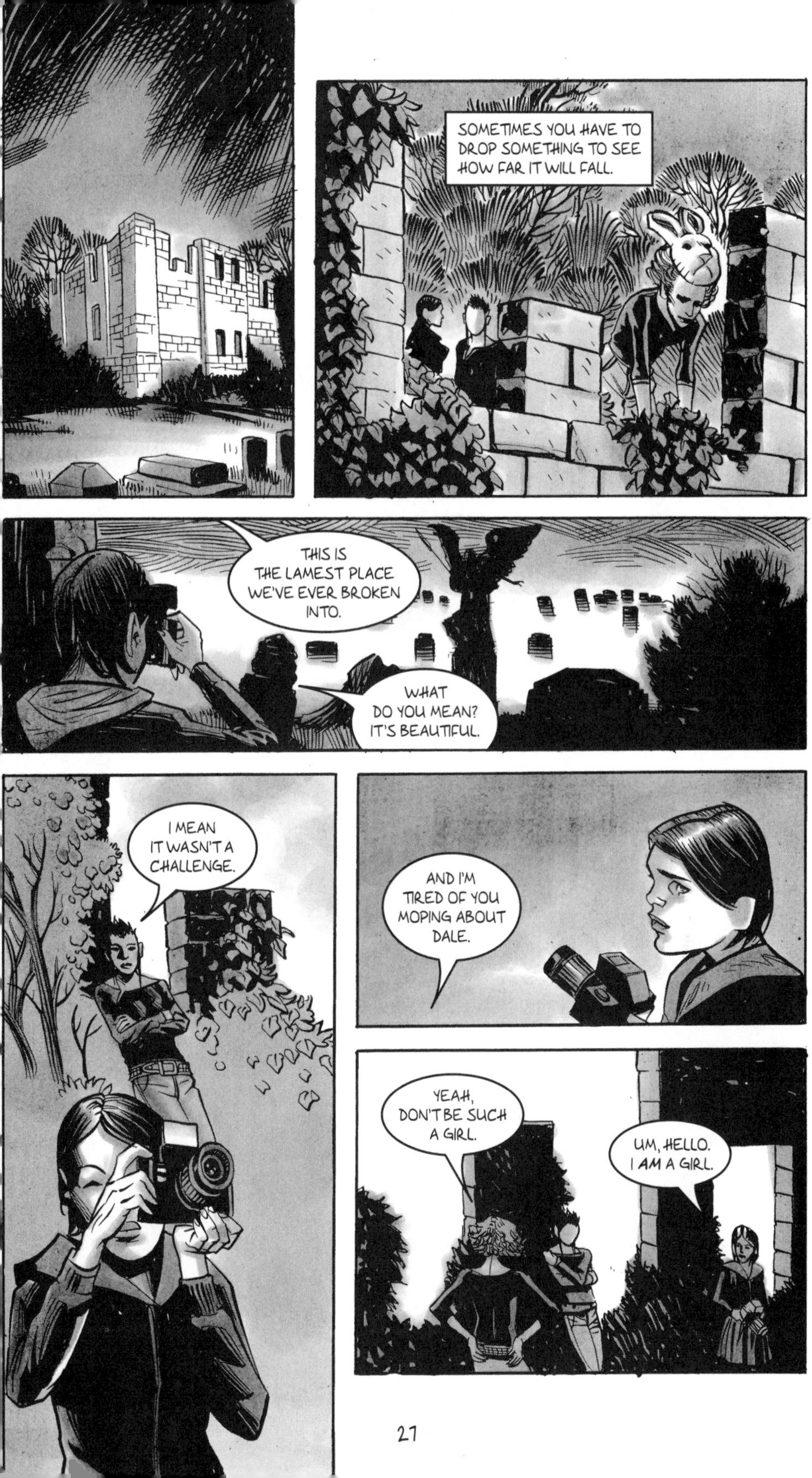
SOMETIMES YOU HAVE TO DROP SOMETHING TO SEE HOW FAR IT WILL FALL.
THIS IS THE LAMEST PLACE WE'VE EVER BROKEN INTO.
WHAT DO YOU MEAN? IT'S BEAUTIFUL.
I MEAN IT WASN'T A CHALLENGE.
AND I'M TIRED OF YOU MOPING ABOUT DALE.
YEAH, DON'T BE SUCH A GIRL.
UM, HELLO. I *AM* A GIRL.

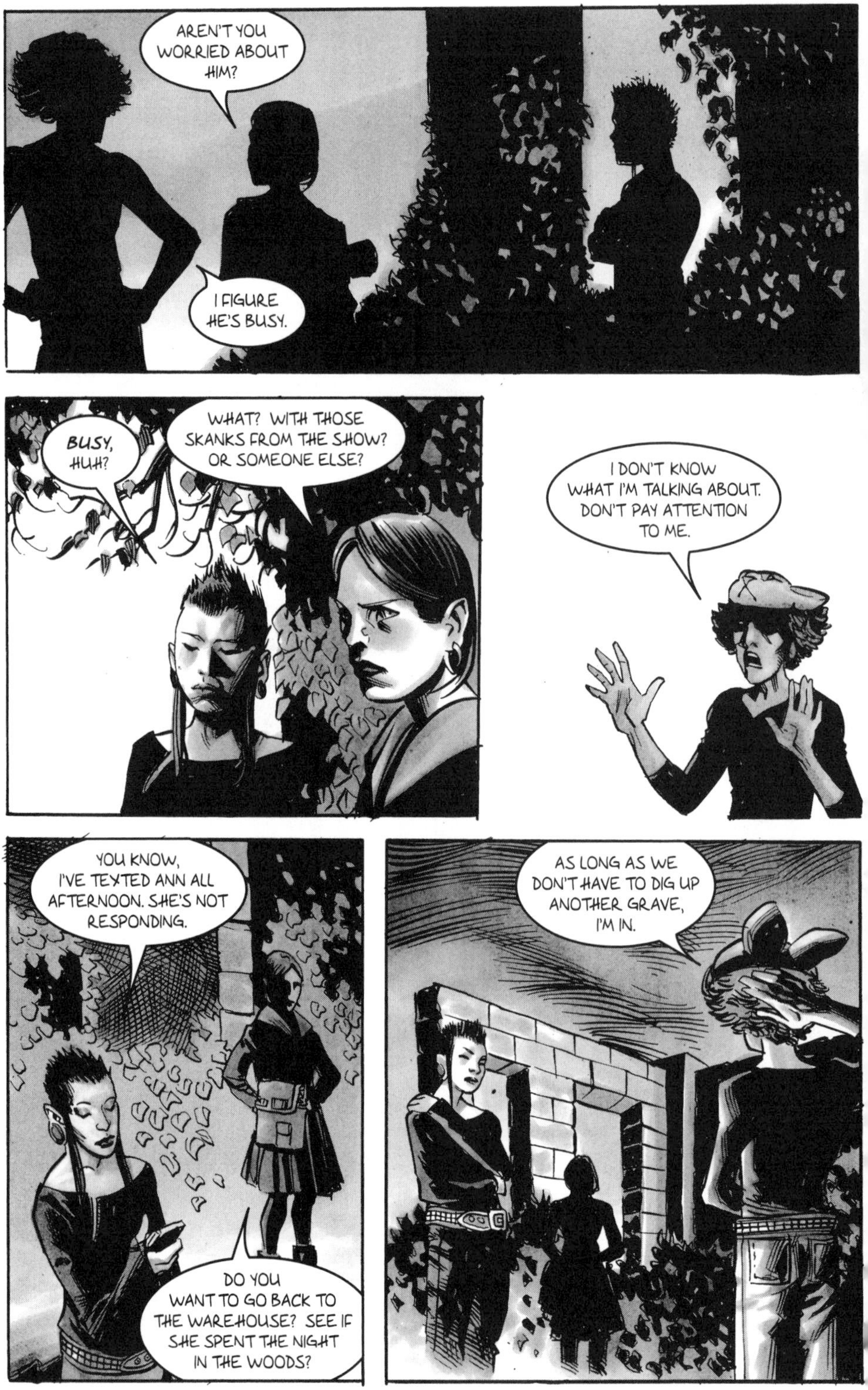
AREN'T YOU WORRIED ABOUT HIM?
I FIGURE HE'S BUSY.
BUSY, HUH?
WHAT? WITH THOSE SKANKS FROM THE SHOW? OR SOMEONE ELSE?
I DON'T KNOW WHAT I'M TALKING ABOUT. DON'T PAY ATTENTION TO ME.
YOU KNOW, I'VE TEXTED ANN ALL AFTERNOON. SHE'S NOT RESPONDING.
DO YOU WANT TO GO BACK TO THE WAREHOUSE? SEE IF SHE SPENT THE NIGHT IN THE WOODS?
AS LONG AS WE DON'T HAVE TO DIG UP ANOTHER GRAVE, I'M IN.

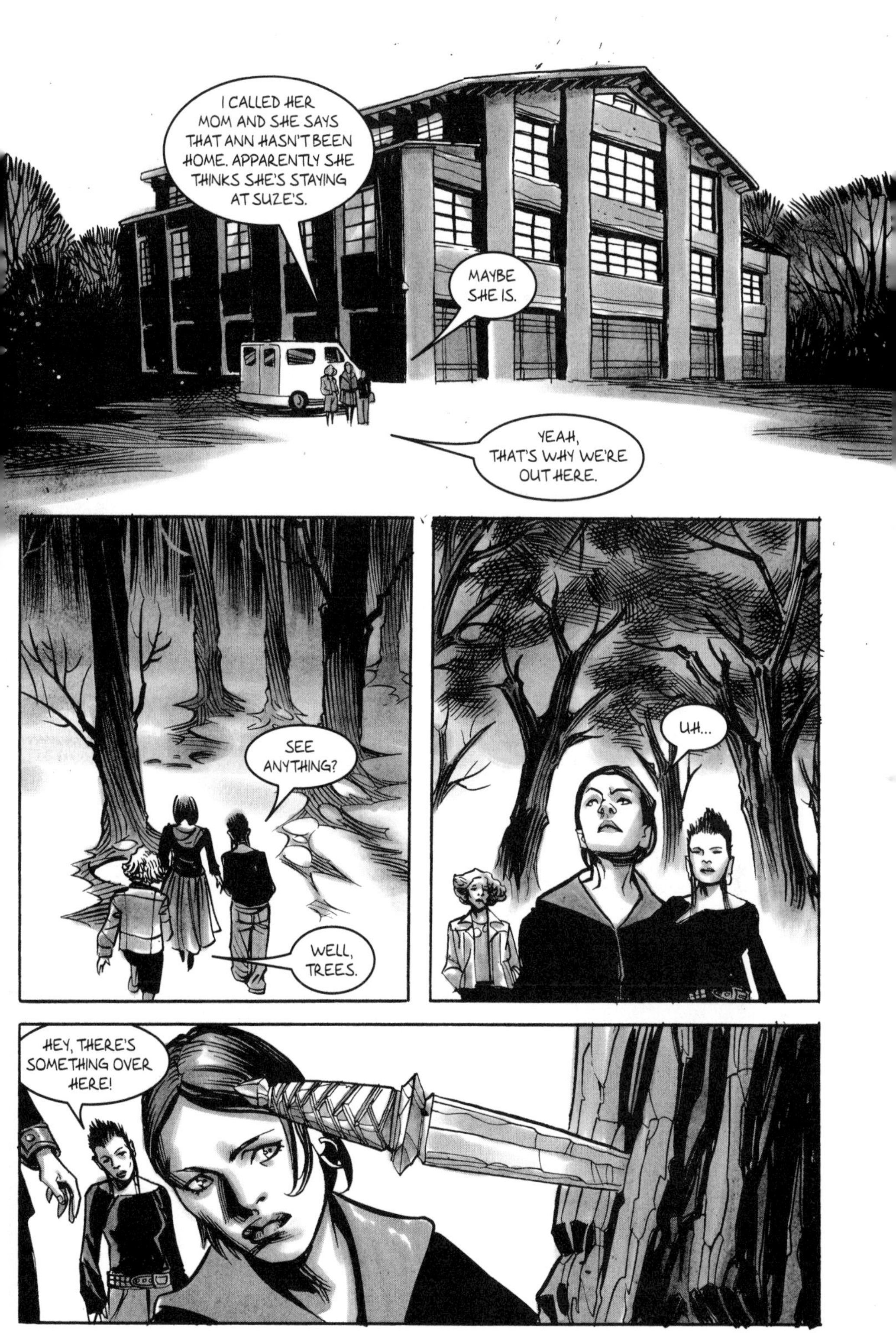
I CALLED HER MOM AND SHE SAYS THAT ANN HASN'T BEEN HOME. APPARENTLY SHE THINKS SHE'S STAYING AT SUZE'S.
MAYBE SHE IS.
YEAH, THAT'S WHY WE'RE OUT HERE.
SEE ANYTHING?
WELL, TREES.
UH...
HEY, THERE'S SOMETHING OVER HERE!

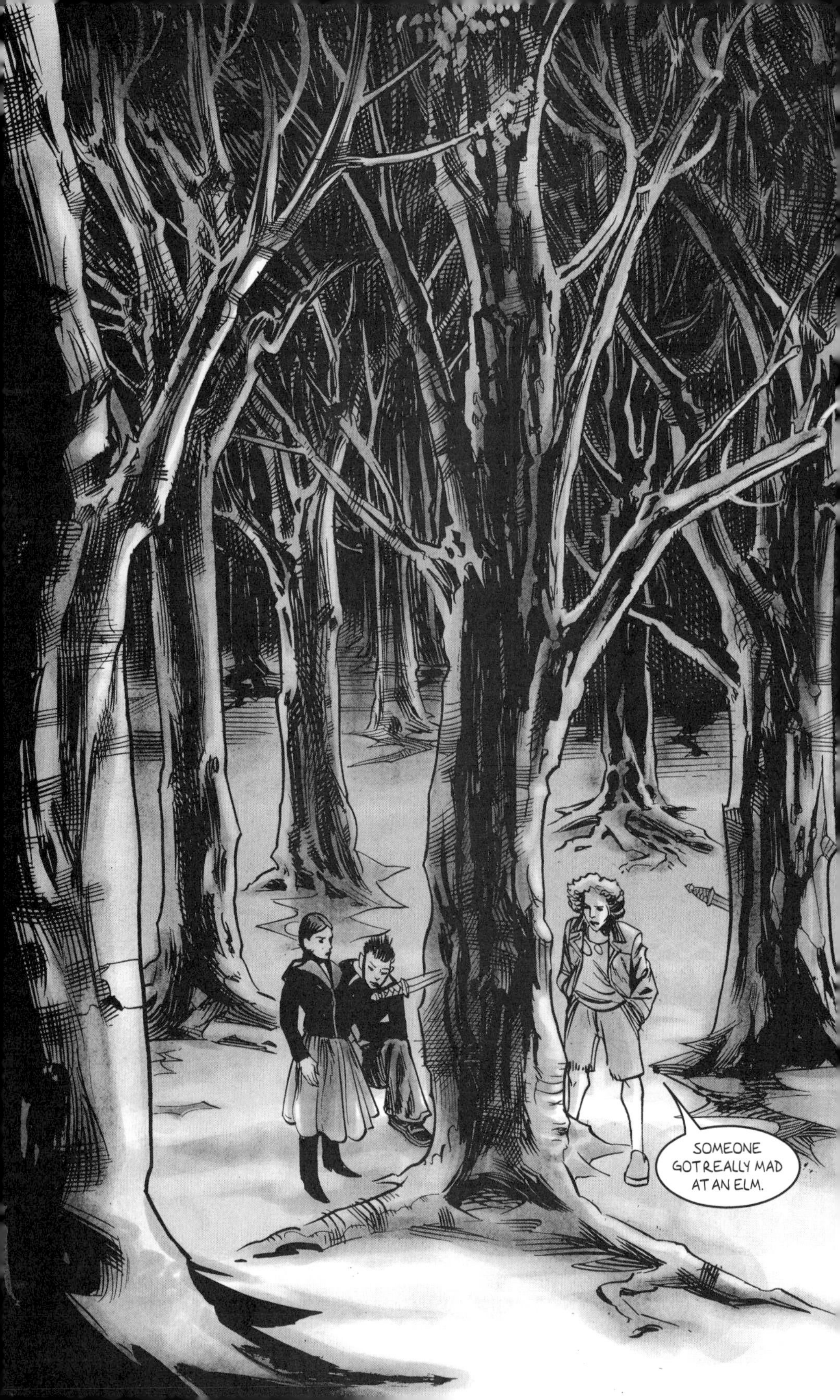
SOMEONE GOT REALLY MAD AT AN ELM.

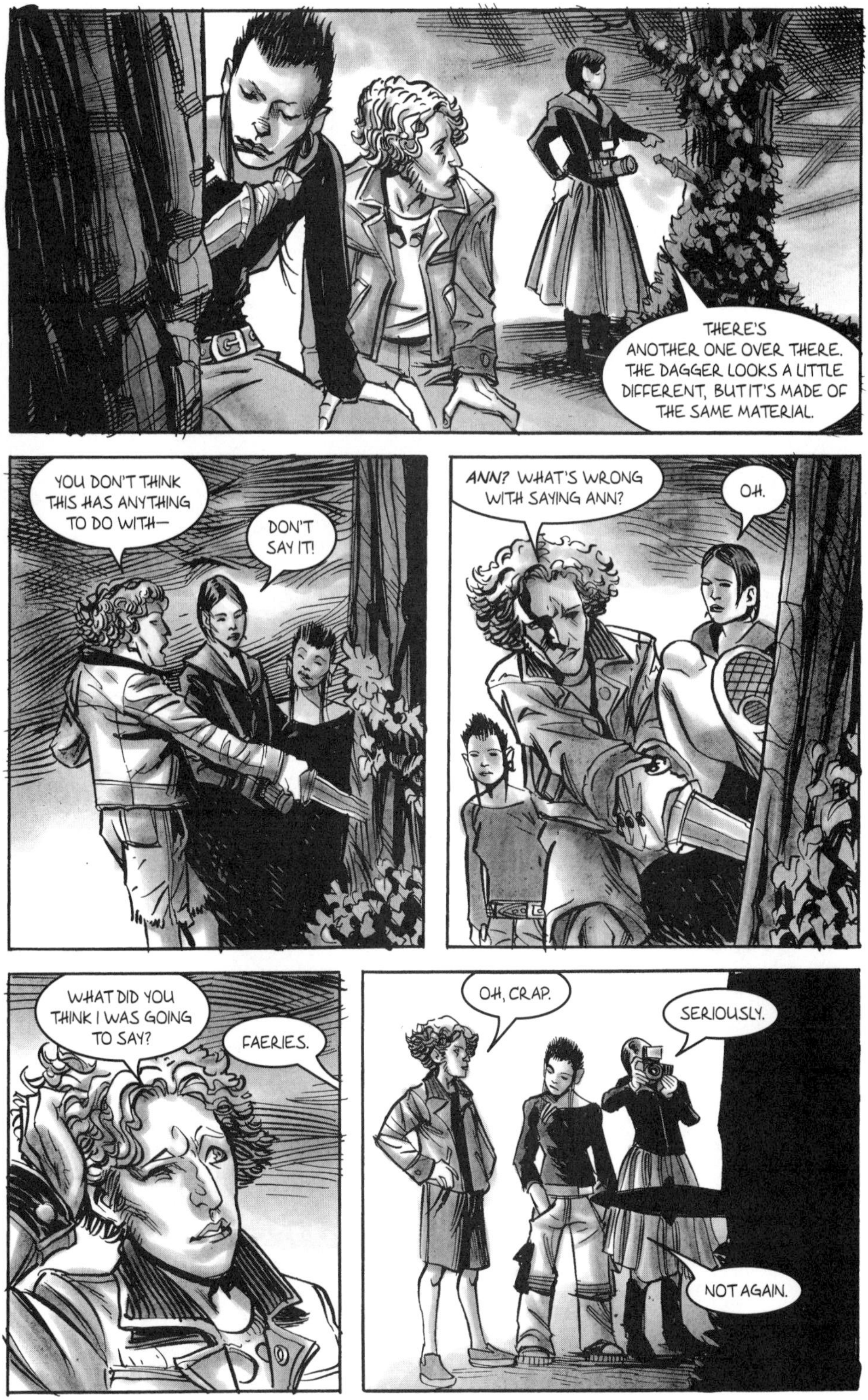
THERE'S ANOTHER ONE OVER THERE. THE DAGGER LOOKS A LITTLE DIFFERENT, BUT IT'S MADE OF THE SAME MATERIAL.
YOU DON'T THINK THIS HAS ANYTHING TO DO WITH—
DON'T SAY IT!
ANN? WHAT'S WRONG WITH SAYING ANN?
OH.
WHAT DID YOU THINK I WAS GOING TO SAY?
FAERIES.
OH, CRAP.
SERIOUSLY.
NOT AGAIN.

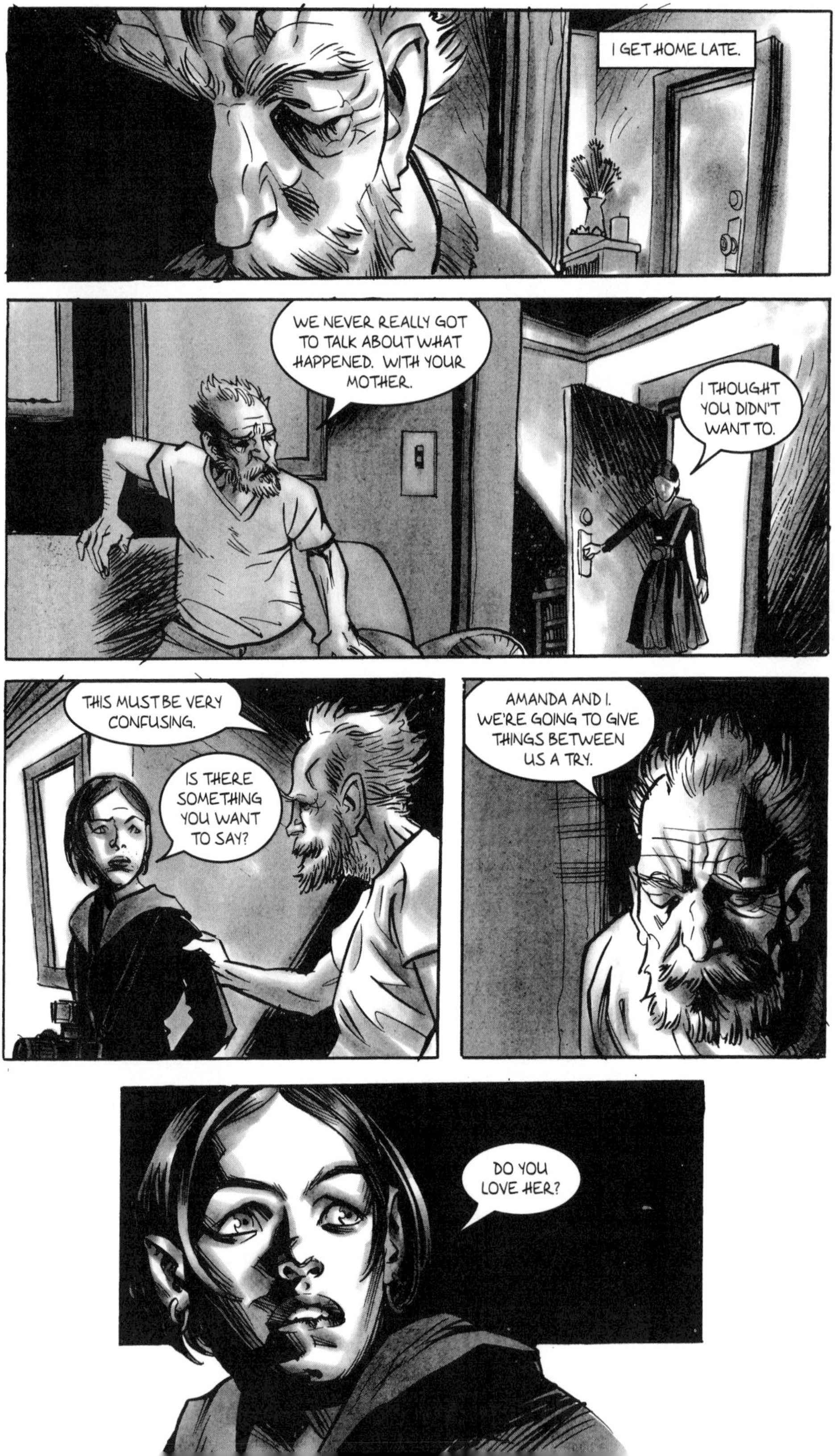
I GET HOME LATE.
WE NEVER REALLY GOT TO TALK ABOUT WHAT HAPPENED. WITH YOUR MOTHER.
I THOUGHT YOU DIDN'T WANT TO.
THIS MUST BE VERY CONFUSING.
IS THERE SOMETHING YOU WANT TO SAY?
AMANDA AND I. WE'RE GOING TO GIVE THINGS BETWEEN US A TRY.
DO YOU LOVE HER?

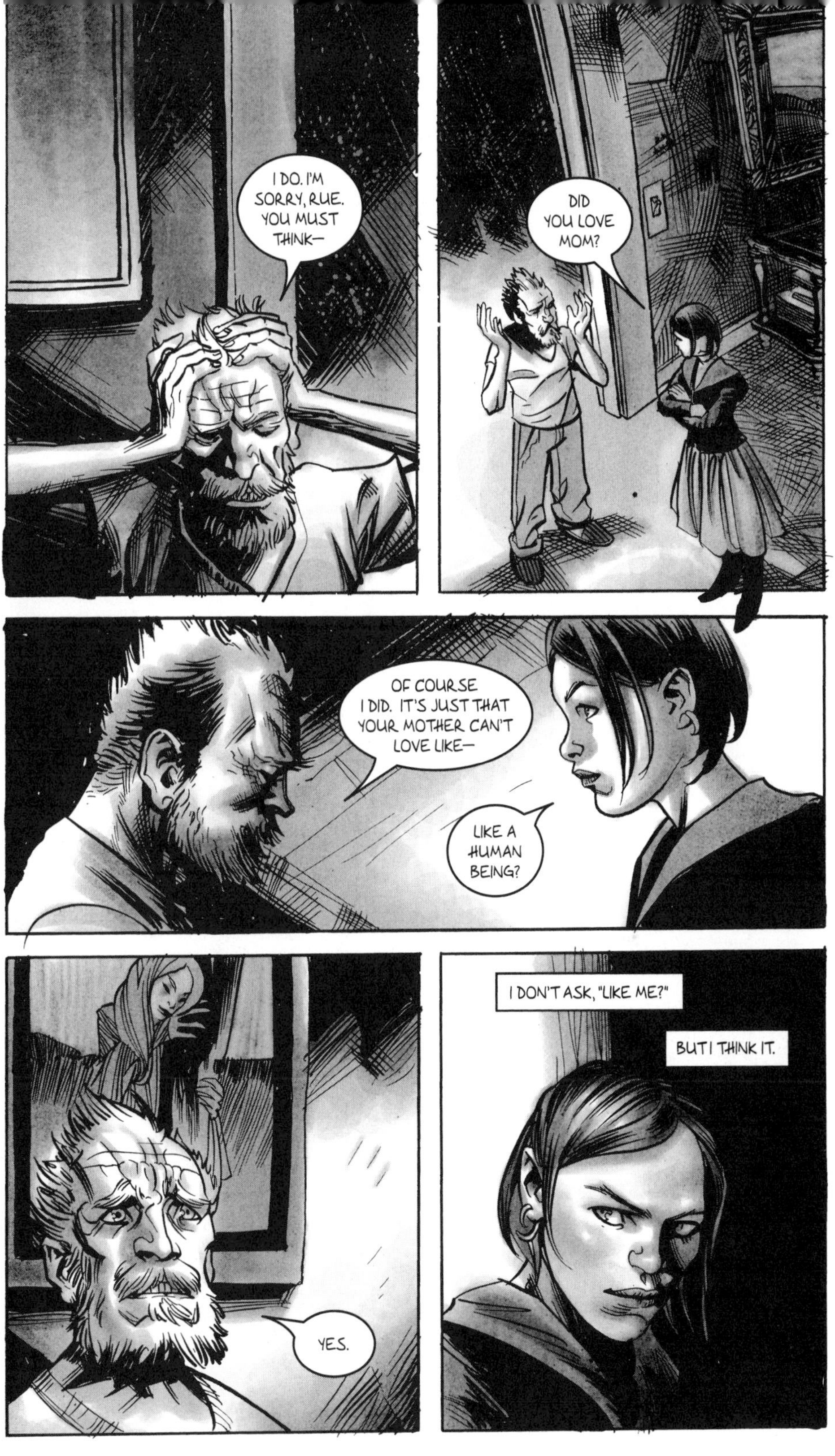
I DO. I'M SORRY, RUE. YOU MUST THINK—
DID YOU LOVE MOM?
OF COURSE I DID. IT'S JUST THAT YOUR MOTHER CAN'T LOVE LIKE—
LIKE A HUMAN BEING?
YES.
I DON'T ASK, "LIKE ME?"
BUT I THINK IT.

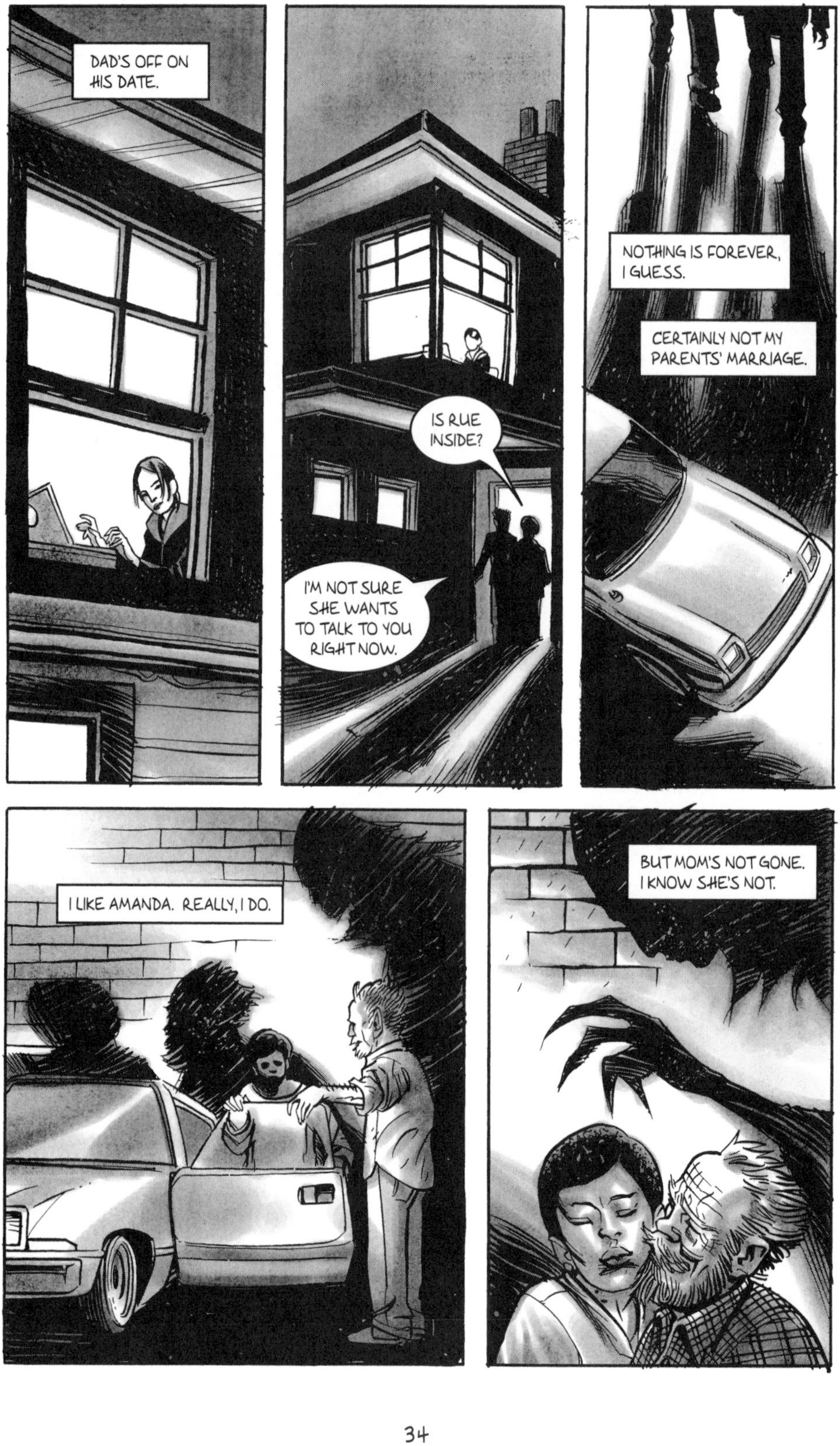
DAD'S OFF ON HIS DATE.
IS RUE INSIDE?
I'M NOT SURE SHE WANTS TO TALK TO YOU RIGHT NOW.
NOTHING IS FOREVER, I GUESS.
CERTAINLY NOT MY PARENTS' MARRIAGE.
I LIKE AMANDA. REALLY, I DO.
BUT MOM'S NOT GONE. I KNOW SHE'S NOT.

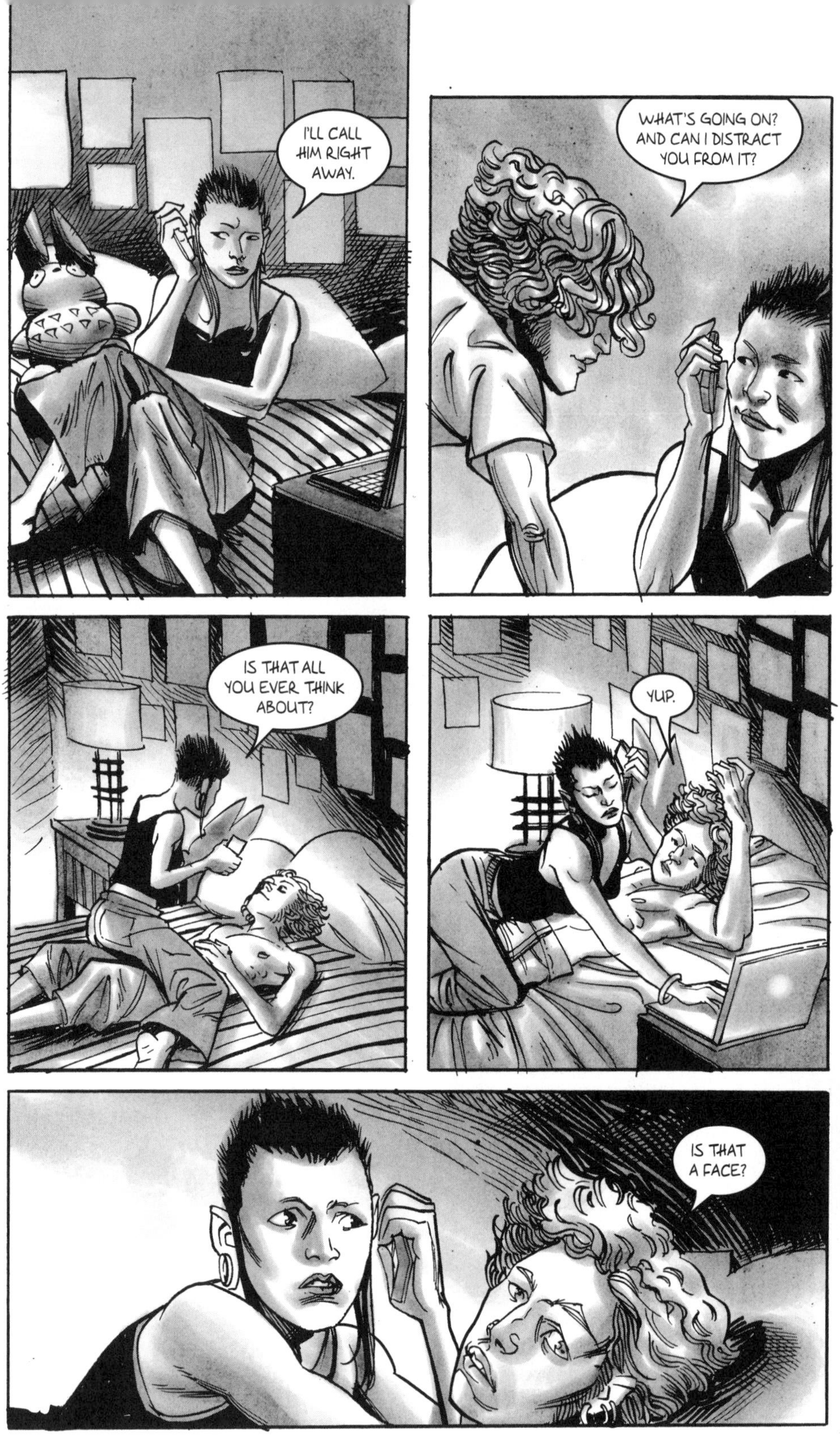
I'LL CALL HIM RIGHT AWAY.
WHAT'S GOING ON? AND CAN I DISTRACT YOU FROM IT?
IS THAT ALL YOU EVER THINK ABOUT?
YUP.
IS THAT A FACE?

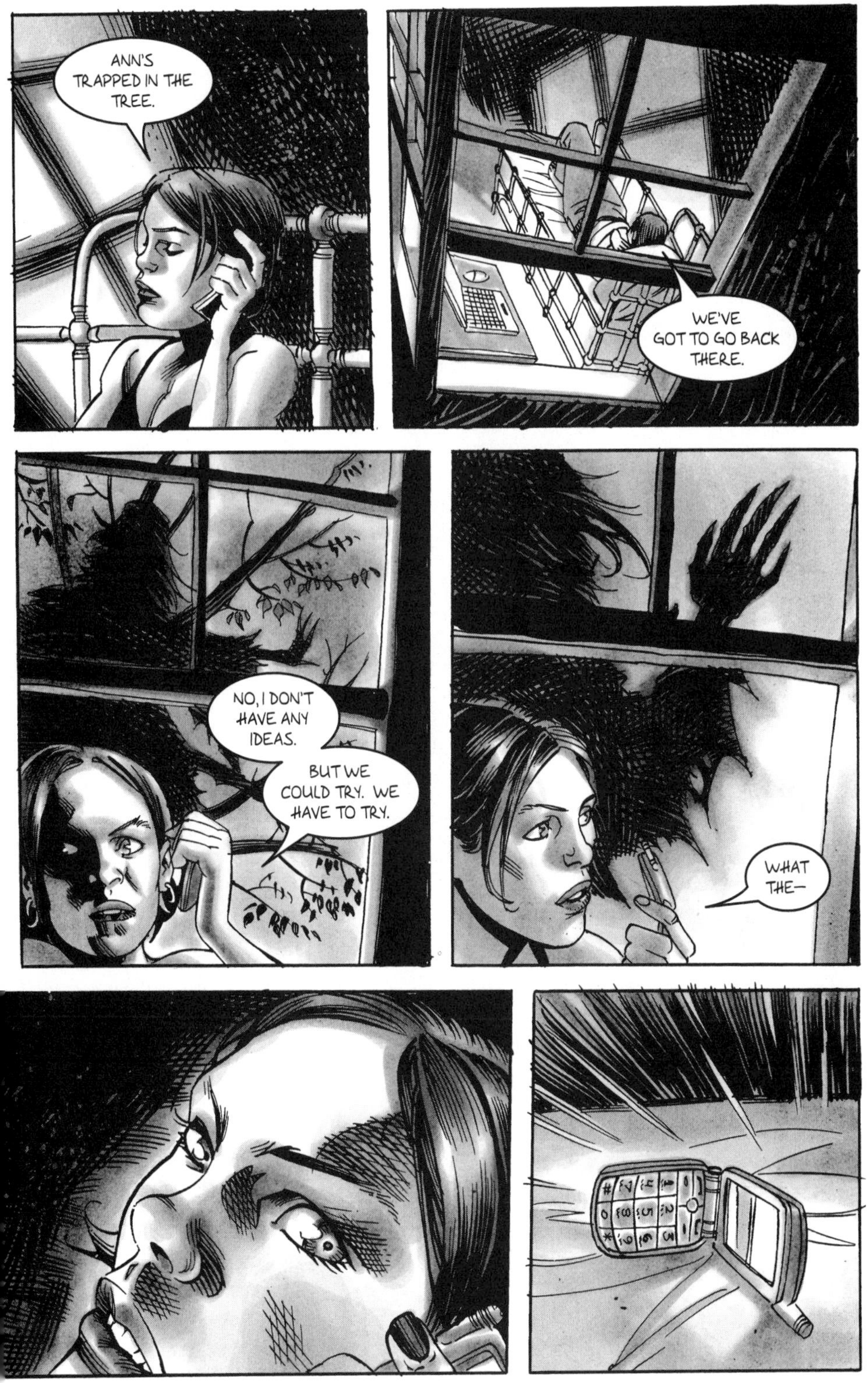
ANN'S TRAPPED IN THE TREE.
WE'VE GOT TO GO BACK THERE.
NO, I DON'T HAVE ANY IDEAS.
BUT WE COULD TRY. WE HAVE TO TRY.
WHAT THE—

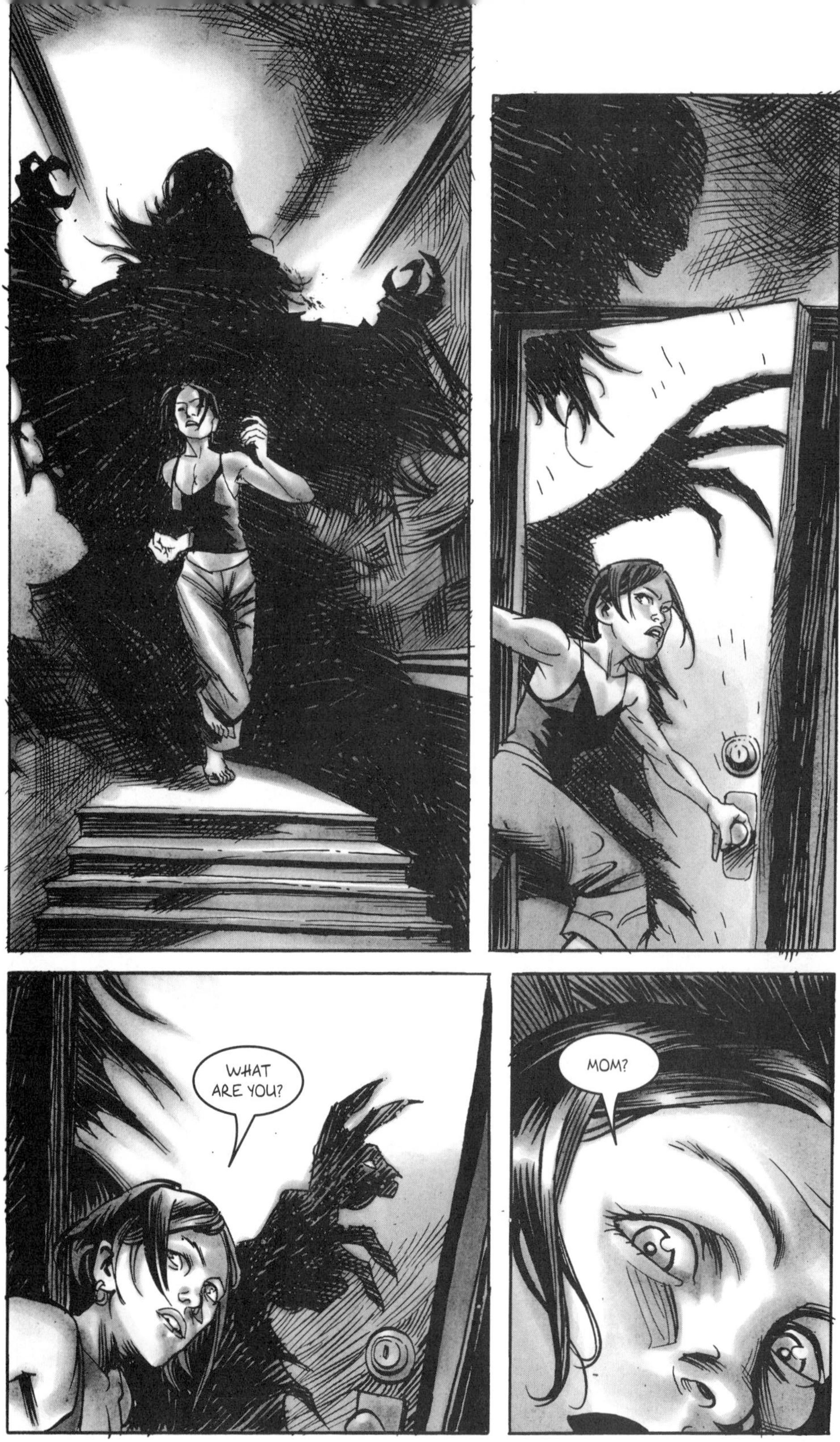
WHAT ARE YOU?
MOM?

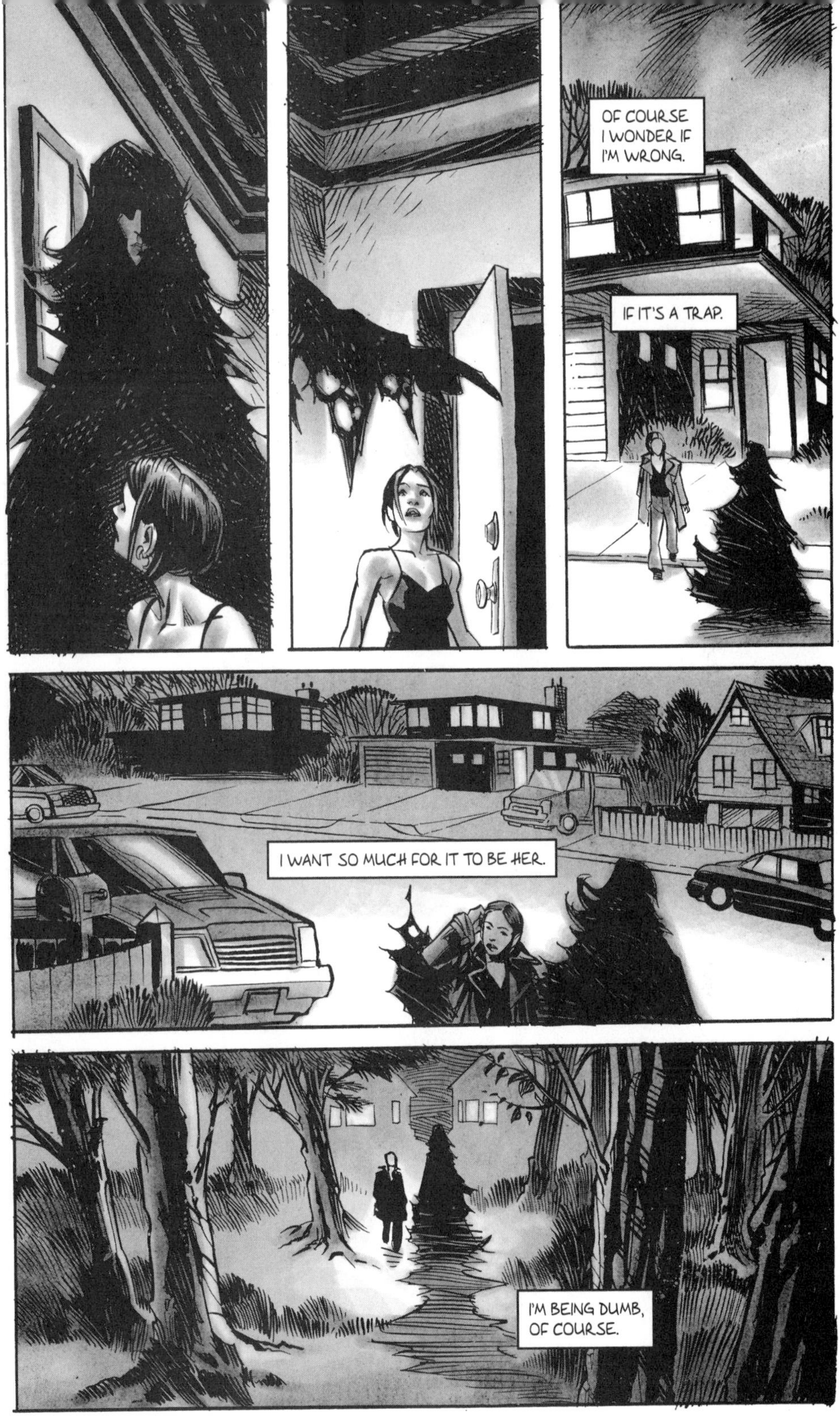
OF COURSE I WONDER IF I'M WRONG.
IF IT'S A TRAP.
I WANT SO MUCH FOR IT TO BE HER.
I'M BEING DUMB, OF COURSE.

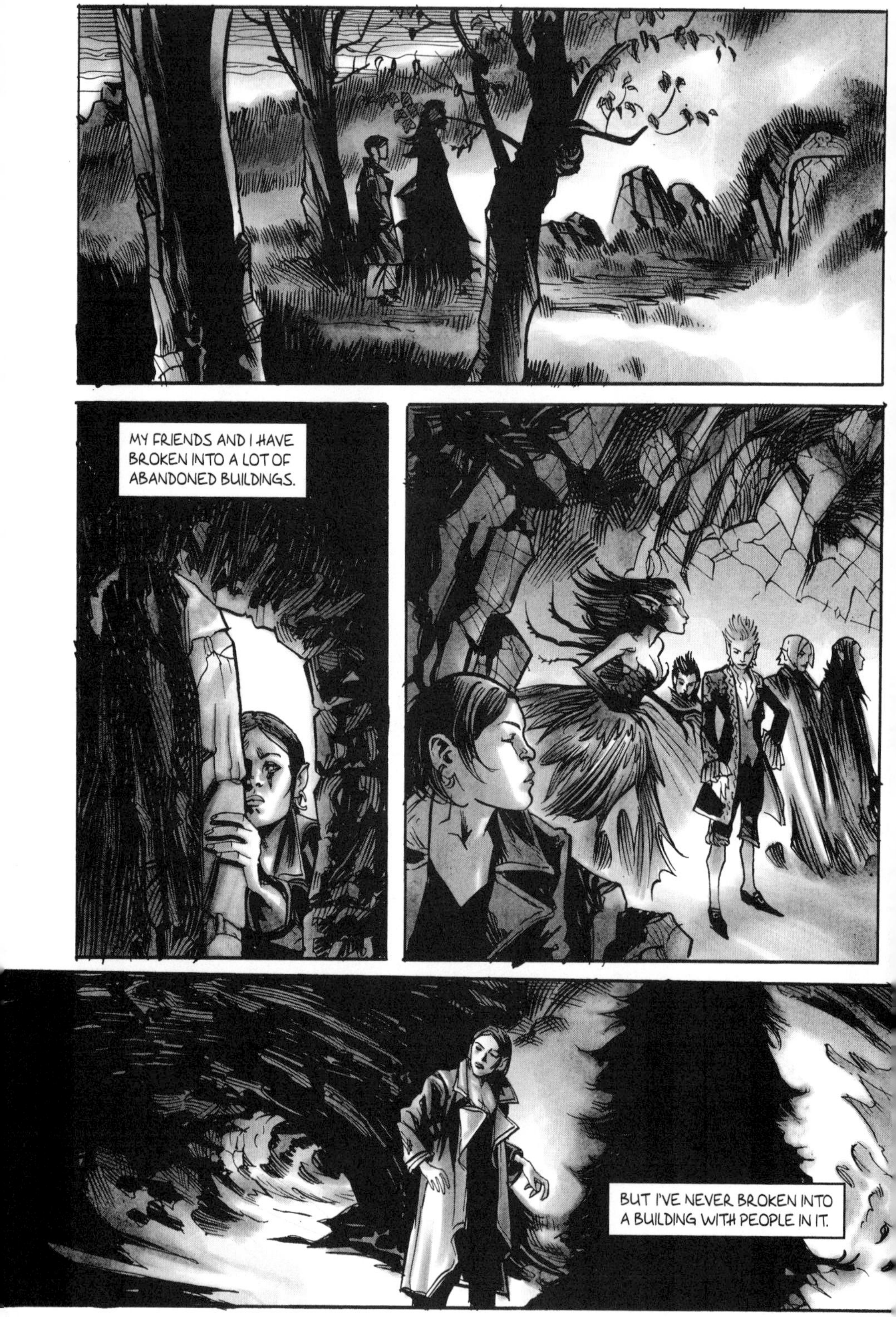
MY FRIENDS AND I HAVE BROKEN INTO A LOT OF ABANDONED BUILDINGS.
BUT I'VE NEVER BROKEN INTO A BUILDING WITH PEOPLE IN IT.

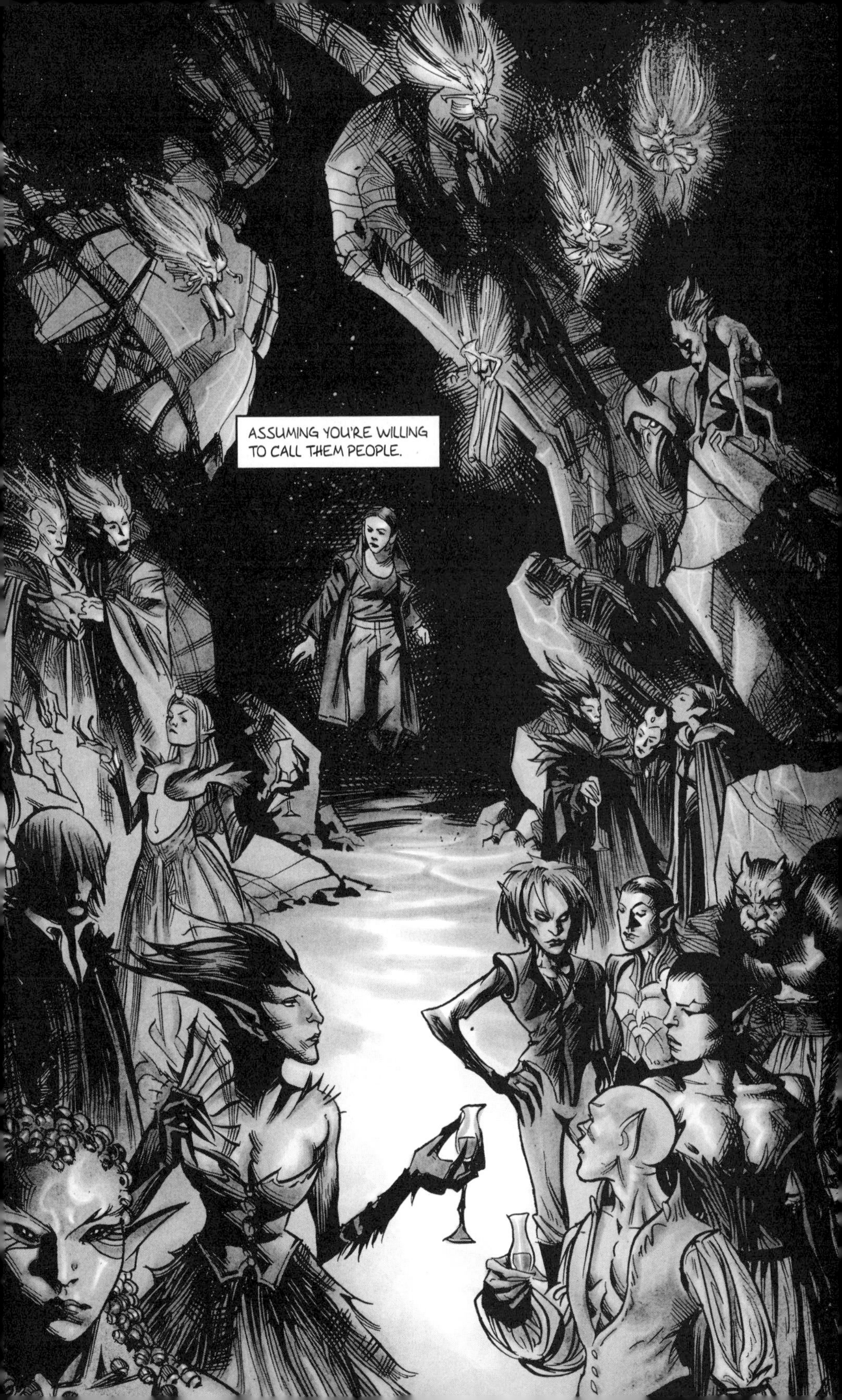
ASSUMING YOU'RE WILLING
TO CALL THEM PEOPLE.

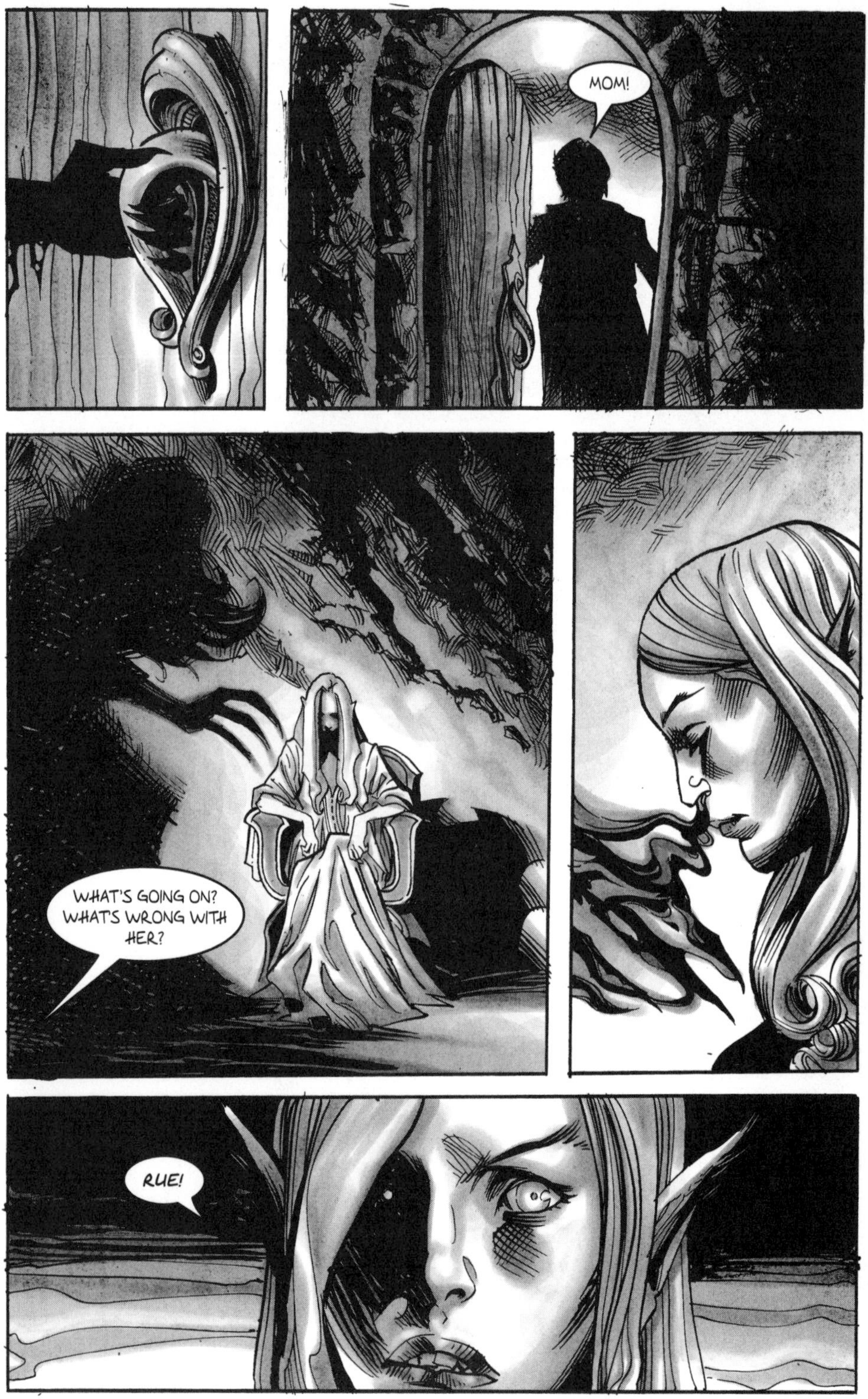
MOM!
WHAT'S GOING ON? WHAT'S WRONG WITH HER?
RUE!

43

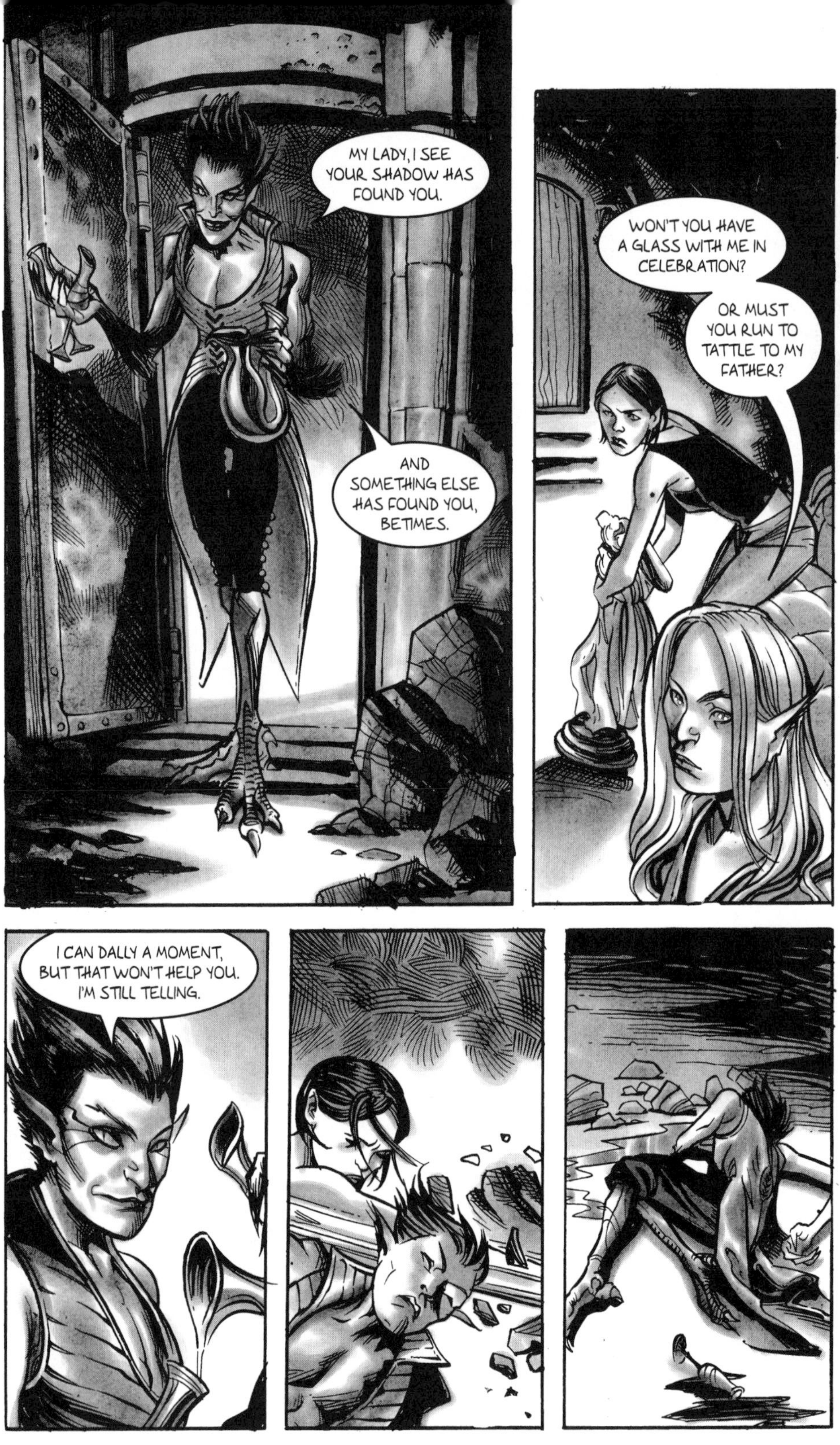
MY LADY, I SEE YOUR SHADOW HAS FOUND YOU.
AND SOMETHING ELSE HAS FOUND YOU, BETIMES.
WON'T YOU HAVE A GLASS WITH ME IN CELEBRATION?
OR MUST YOU RUN TO TATTLE TO MY FATHER?
I CAN DALLY A MOMENT, BUT THAT WON'T HELP YOU. I'M STILL TELLING.

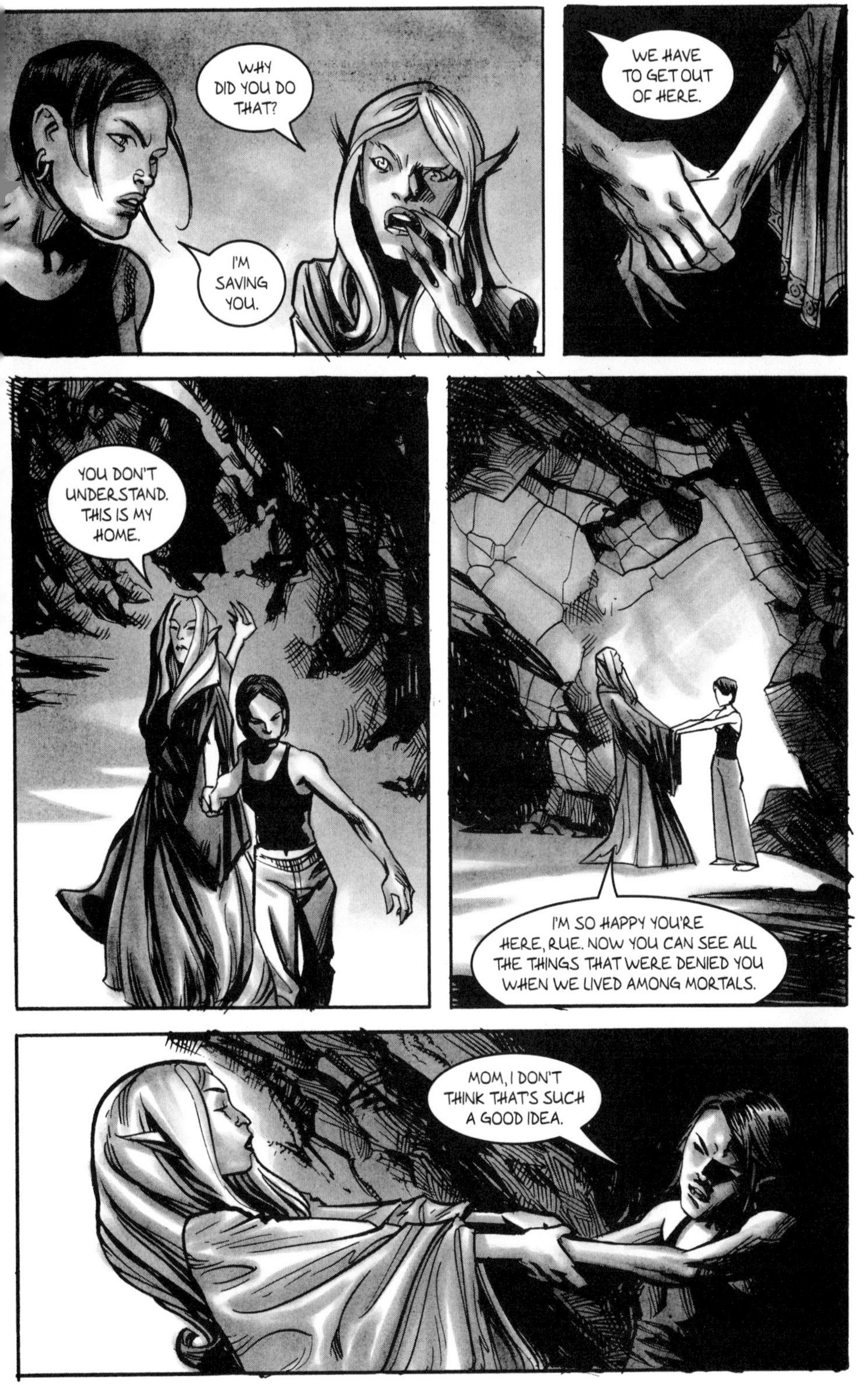
WHY DID YOU DO THAT?
I'M SAVING YOU.
WE HAVE TO GET OUT OF HERE.
YOU DON'T UNDERSTAND. THIS IS MY HOME.
I'M SO HAPPY YOU'RE HERE, RUE. NOW YOU CAN SEE ALL THE THINGS THAT WERE DENIED YOU WHEN WE LIVED AMONG MORTALS.
MOM, I DON'T THINK THAT'S SUCH A GOOD IDEA.

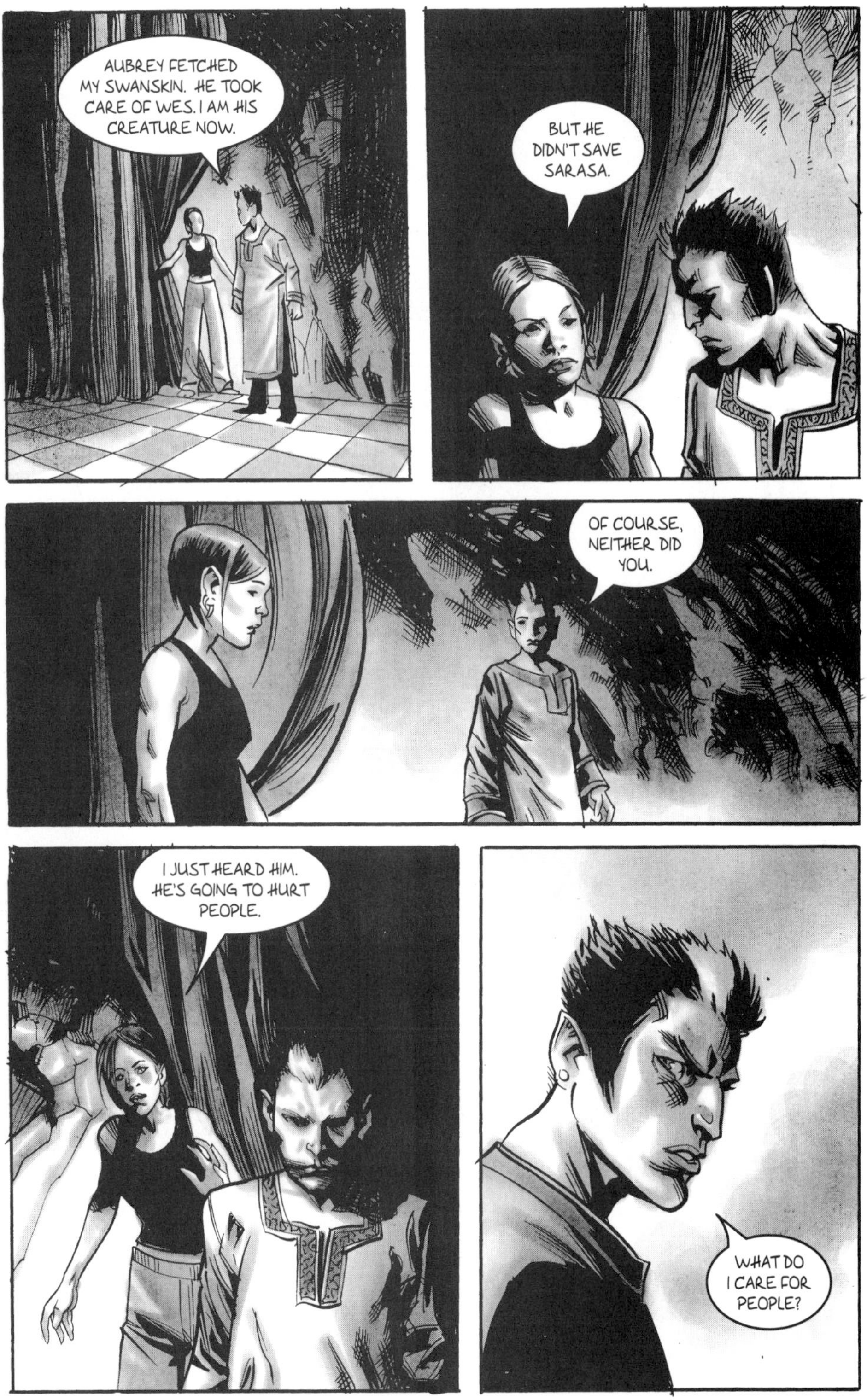
AUBREY FETCHED MY SWANSKIN. HE TOOK CARE OF WES. I AM HIS CREATURE NOW.
BUT HE DIDN'T SAVE SARASA.
OF COURSE, NEITHER DID YOU.
I JUST HEARD HIM. HE'S GOING TO HURT PEOPLE.
WHAT DO I CARE FOR PEOPLE?

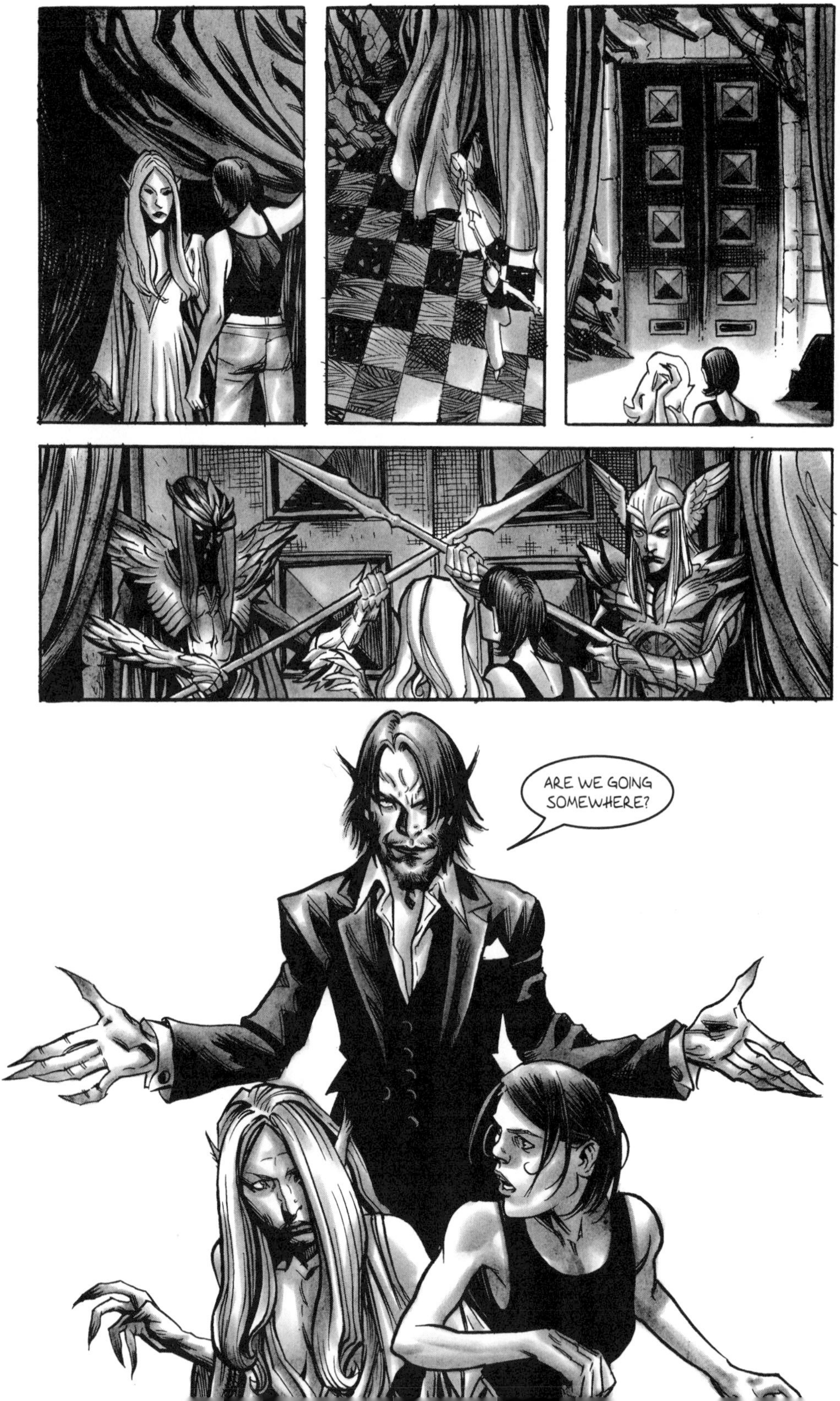
ARE WE GOING SOMEWHERE?

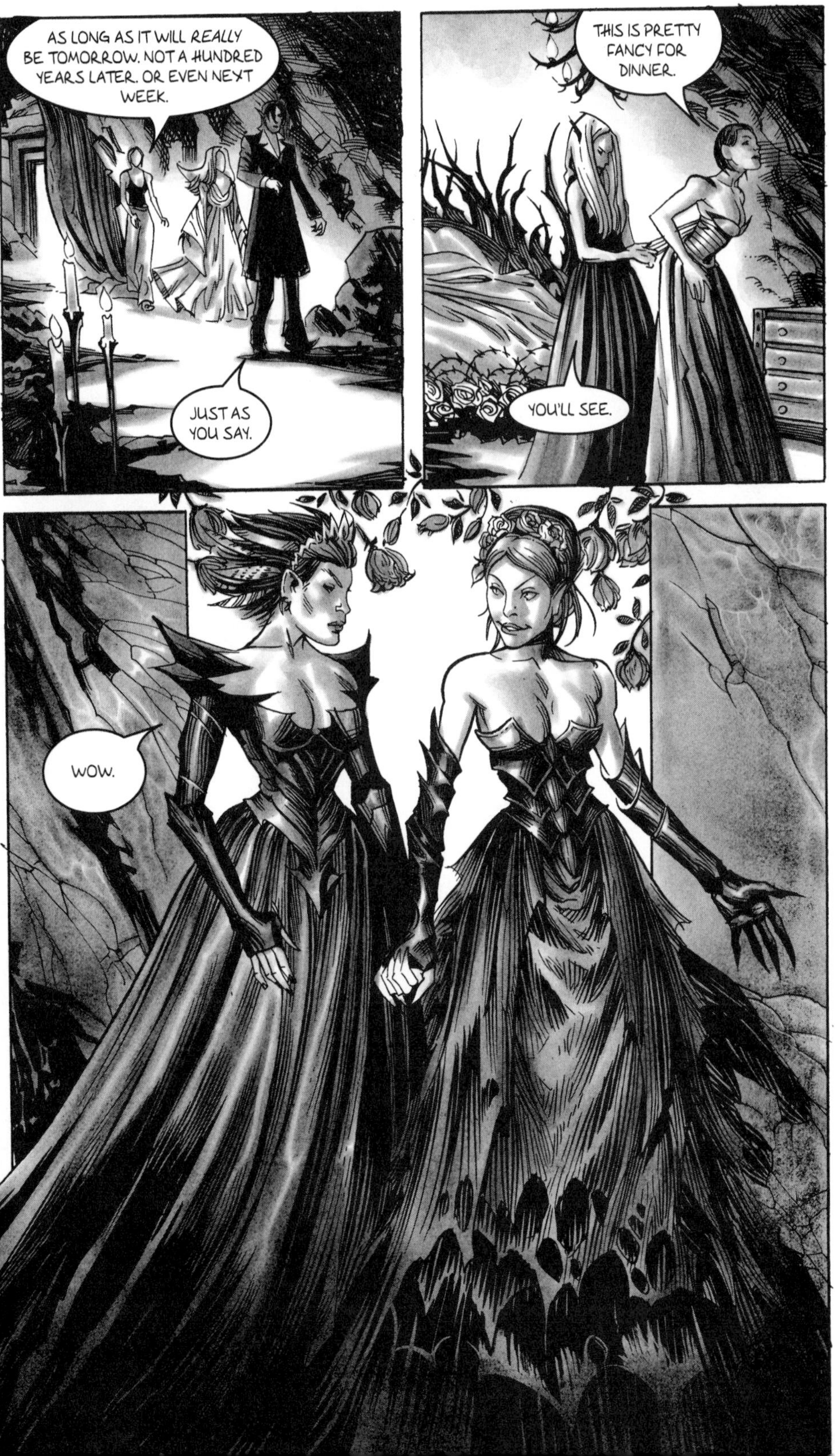
AS LONG AS IT WILL REALLY BE TOMORROW. NOT A HUNDRED YEARS LATER. OR EVEN NEXT WEEK.
JUST AS YOU SAY.
THIS IS PRETTY FANCY FOR DINNER.
YOU'LL SEE.
WOW.

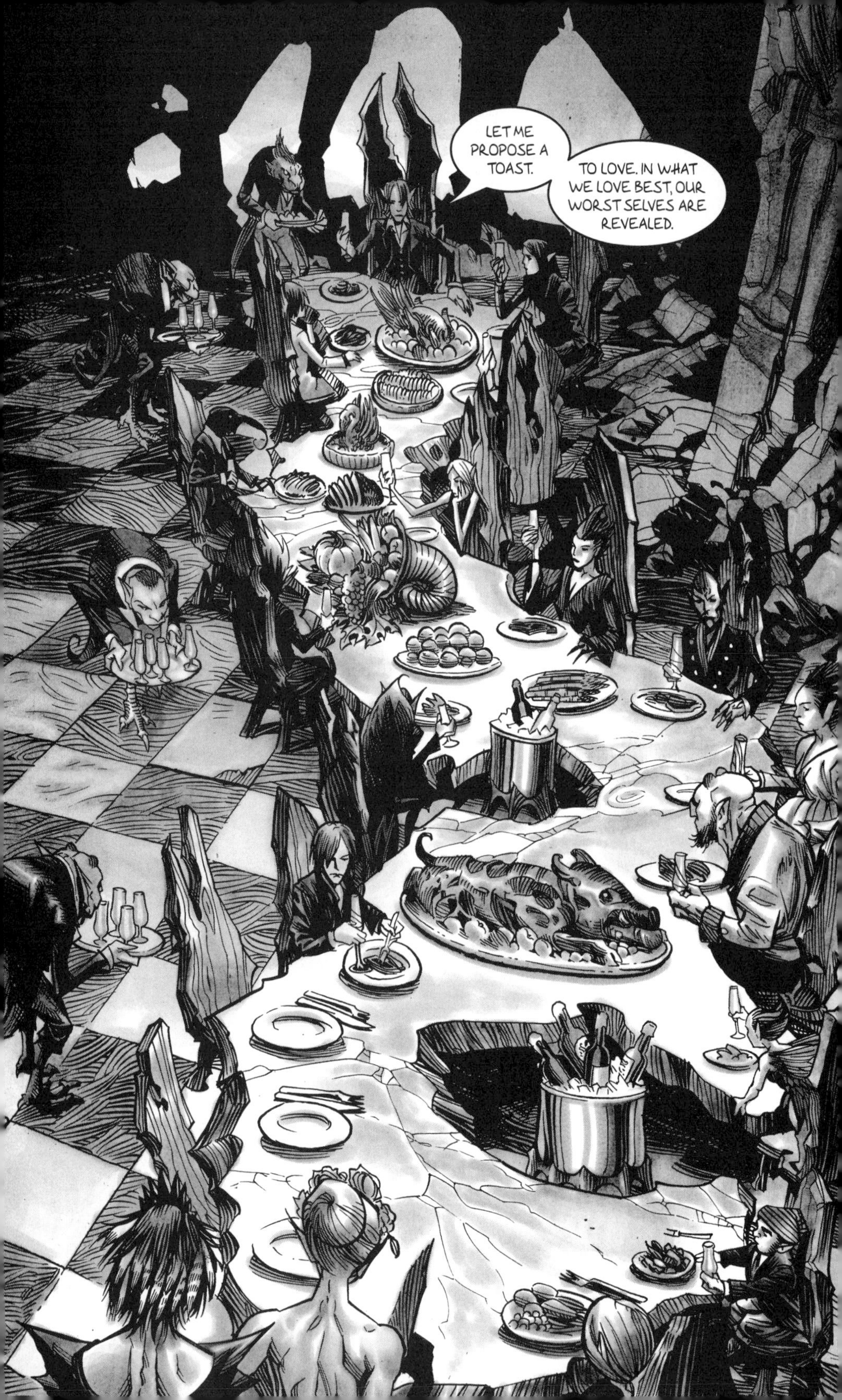
LET ME PROPOSE A TOAST.
TO LOVE. IN WHAT WE LOVE BEST, OUR WORST SELVES ARE REVEALED.

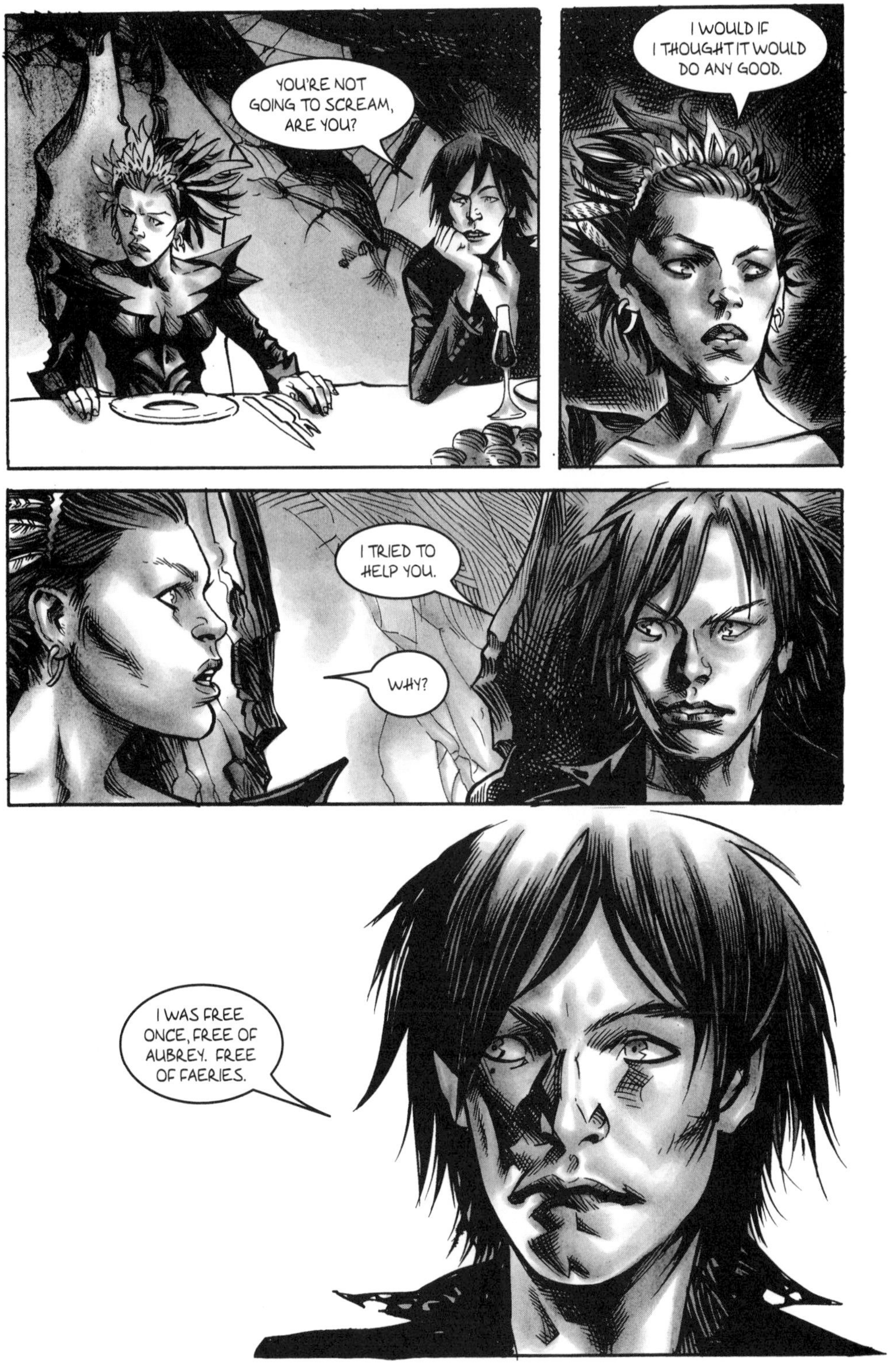
YOU'RE NOT GOING TO SCREAM, ARE YOU?
I WOULD IF I THOUGHT IT WOULD DO ANY GOOD.
I TRIED TO HELP YOU.
WHY?
I WAS FREE ONCE, FREE OF AUBREY. FREE OF FAERIES.

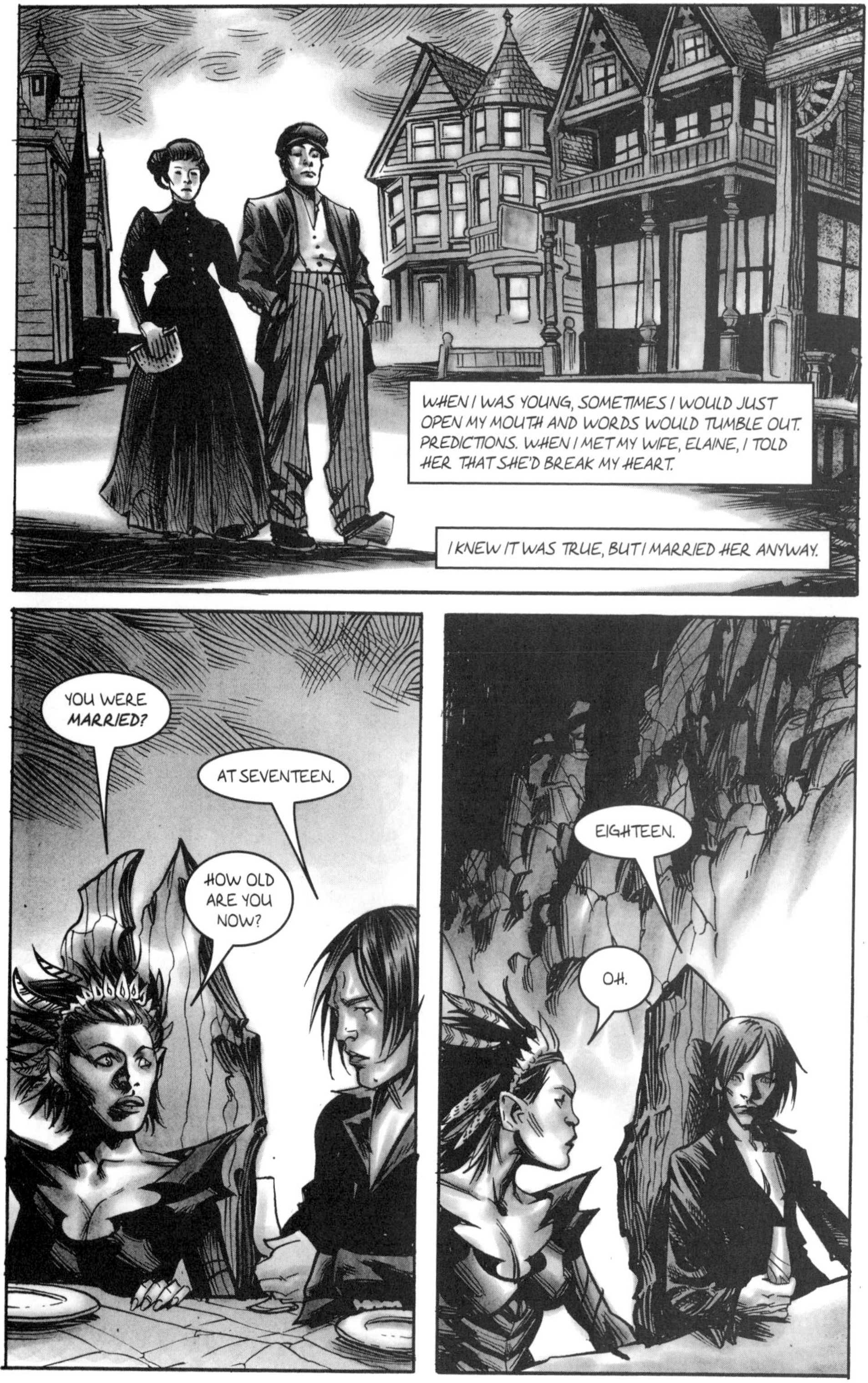
WHEN I WAS YOUNG, SOMETIMES I WOULD JUST OPEN MY MOUTH AND WORDS WOULD TUMBLE OUT. PREDICTIONS. WHEN I MET MY WIFE, ELAINE, I TOLD HER THAT SHE'D BREAK MY HEART.
I KNEW IT WAS TRUE, BUT I MARRIED HER ANYWAY.
YOU WERE MARRIED?
AT SEVENTEEN.
HOW OLD ARE YOU NOW?
EIGHTEEN.
OH.

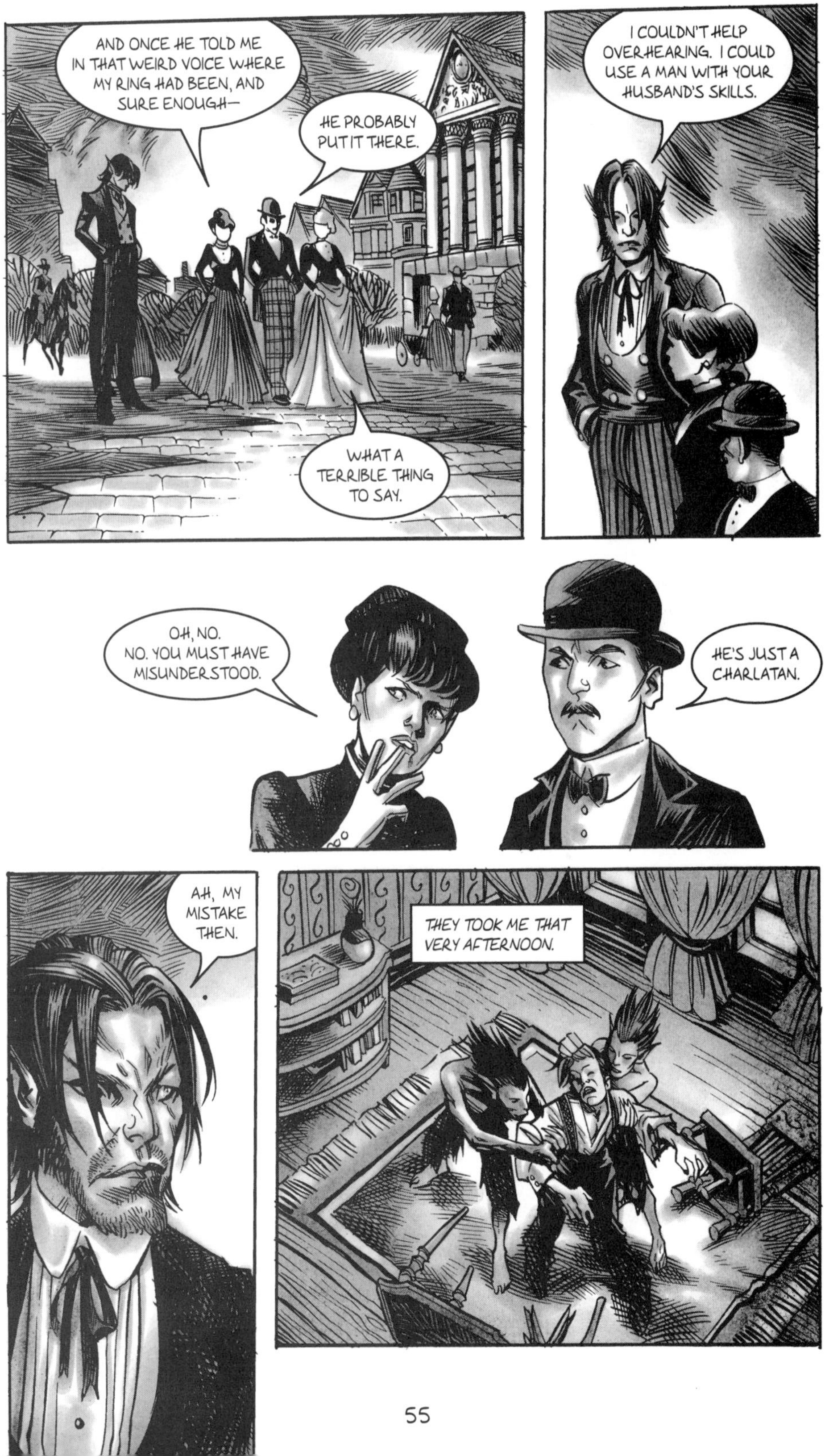
AND ONCE HE TOLD ME IN THAT WEIRD VOICE WHERE MY RING HAD BEEN, AND SURE ENOUGH—
HE PROBABLY PUT IT THERE.
WHAT A TERRIBLE THING TO SAY.
I COULDN'T HELP OVERHEARING. I COULD USE A MAN WITH YOUR HUSBAND'S SKILLS.
OH, NO. NO. YOU MUST HAVE MISUNDERSTOOD.
HE'S JUST A CHARLATAN.
AH, MY MISTAKE THEN.
THEY TOOK ME THAT VERY AFTERNOON.

58

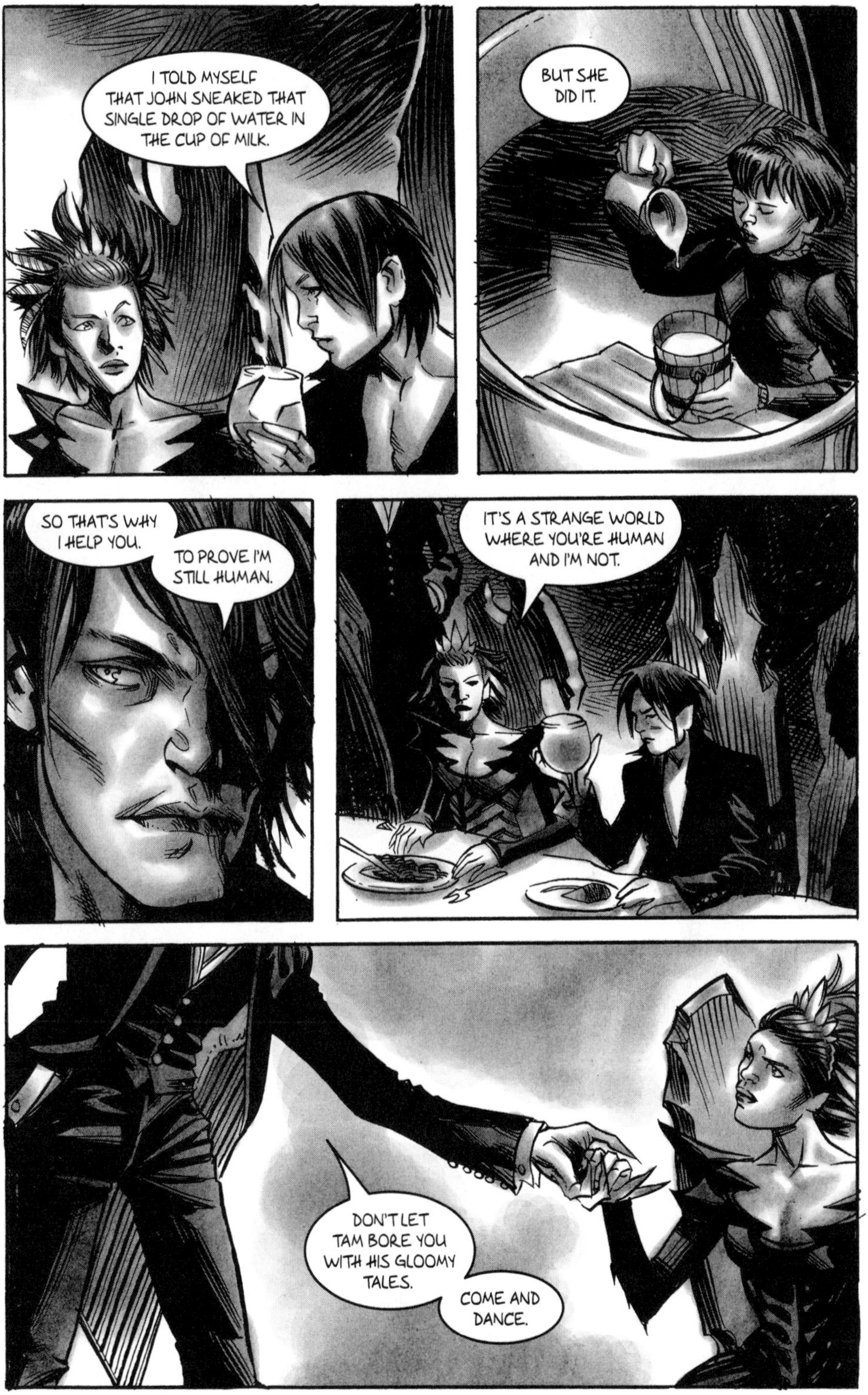
I TOLD MYSELF THAT JOHN SNEAKED THAT SINGLE DROP OF WATER IN THE CUP OF MILK.
BUT SHE DID IT.
SO THAT'S WHY I HELP YOU.
TO PROVE I'M STILL HUMAN.
IT'S A STRANGE WORLD WHERE YOU'RE HUMAN AND I'M NOT.
DON'T LET TAM BORE YOU WITH HIS GLOOMY TALES.
COME AND DANCE.

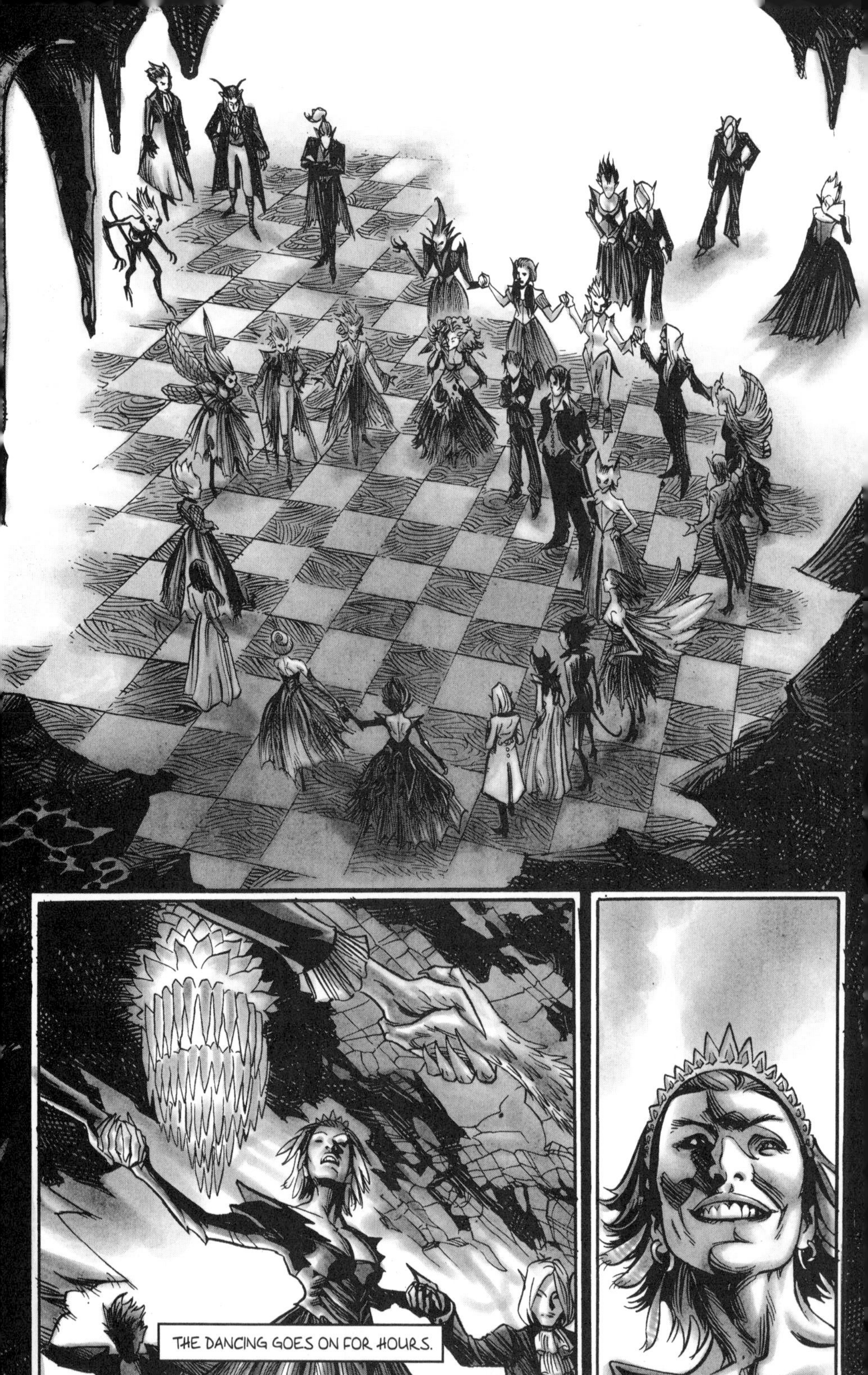
THE DANCING GOES ON FOR HOURS.

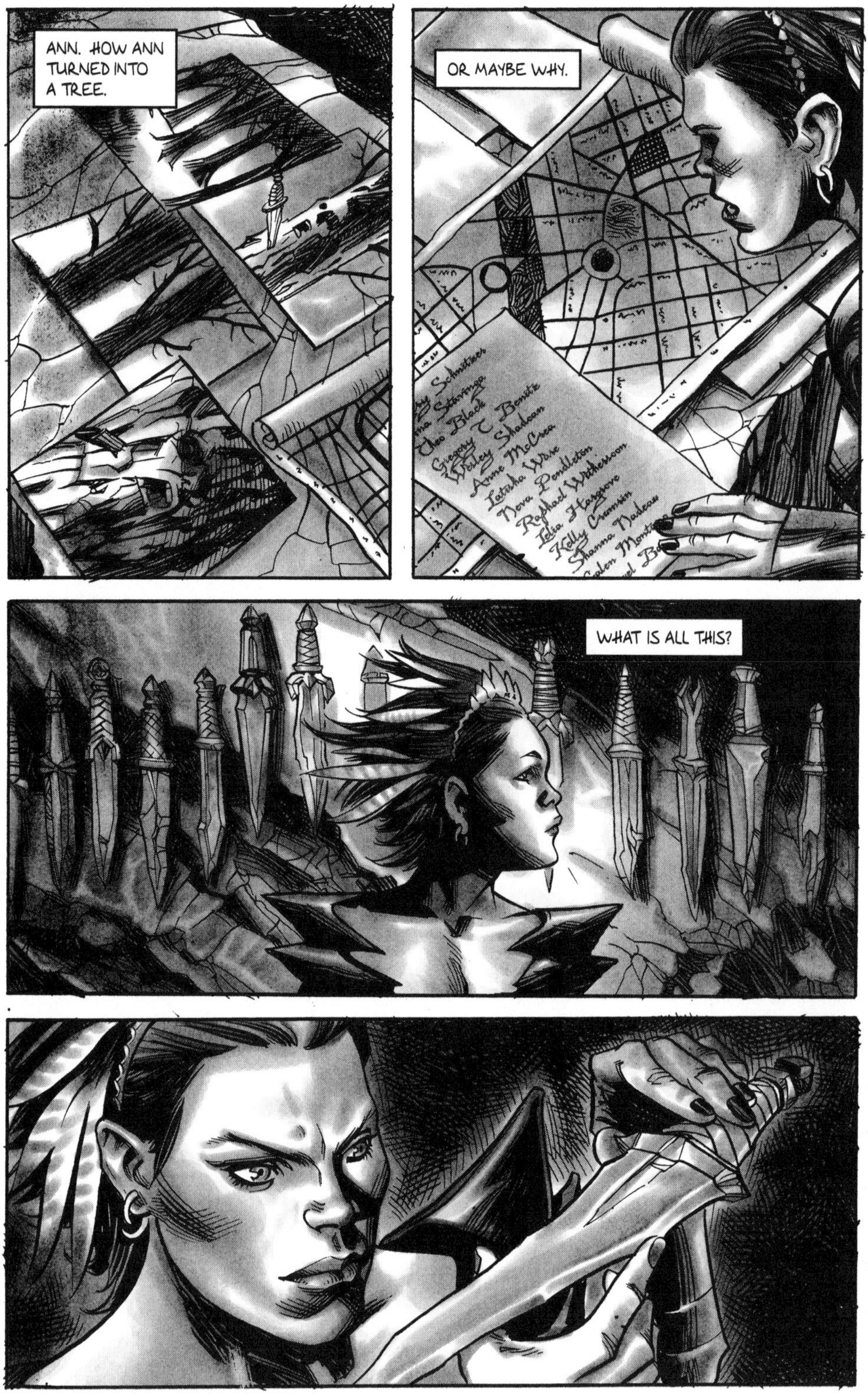
ANN. HOW ANN TURNED INTO A TREE.
OR MAYBE WHY.
Cheo Black
Gregory T. Benitez
Wesley Shadoan
Anne McCrea
Latasha Ware
Nova Pendleton
Raphael Witherspoon
Lelia Hargrove
Kelly Cremin
Shanna Nadeau
WHAT IS ALL THIS?

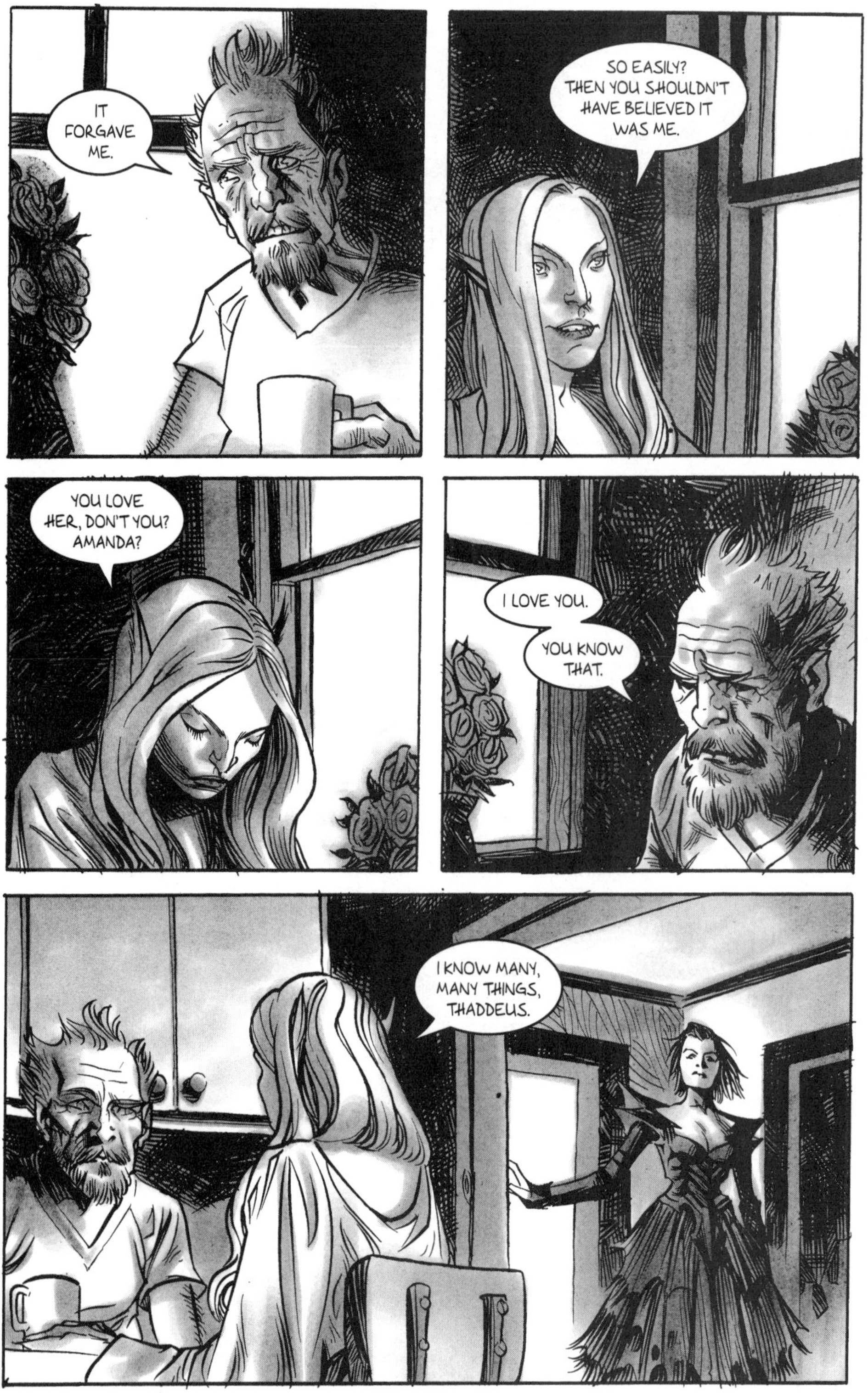
IT FORGAVE ME.
SO EASILY? THEN YOU SHOULDN'T HAVE BELIEVED IT WAS ME.
YOU LOVE HER, DON'T YOU? AMANDA?
I LOVE YOU.
YOU KNOW THAT.
I KNOW MANY, MANY THINGS, THADDEUS.

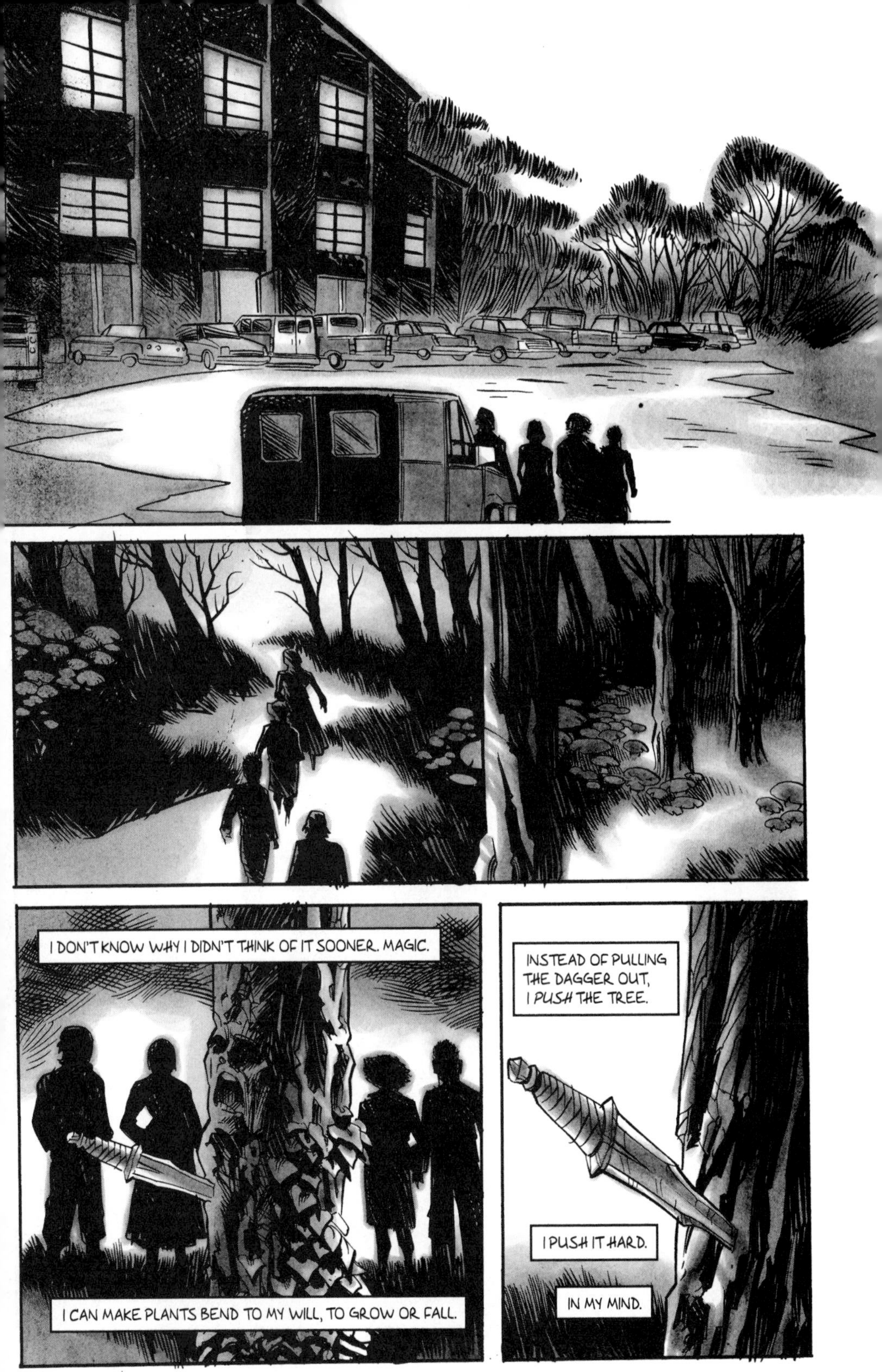
I DON'T KNOW WHY I DIDN'T THINK OF IT SOONER. MAGIC.
I CAN MAKE PLANTS BEND TO MY WILL, TO GROW OR FALL.
INSTEAD OF PULLING THE DAGGER OUT, I *PUSH* THE TREE.
I PUSH IT HARD.
IN MY MIND.

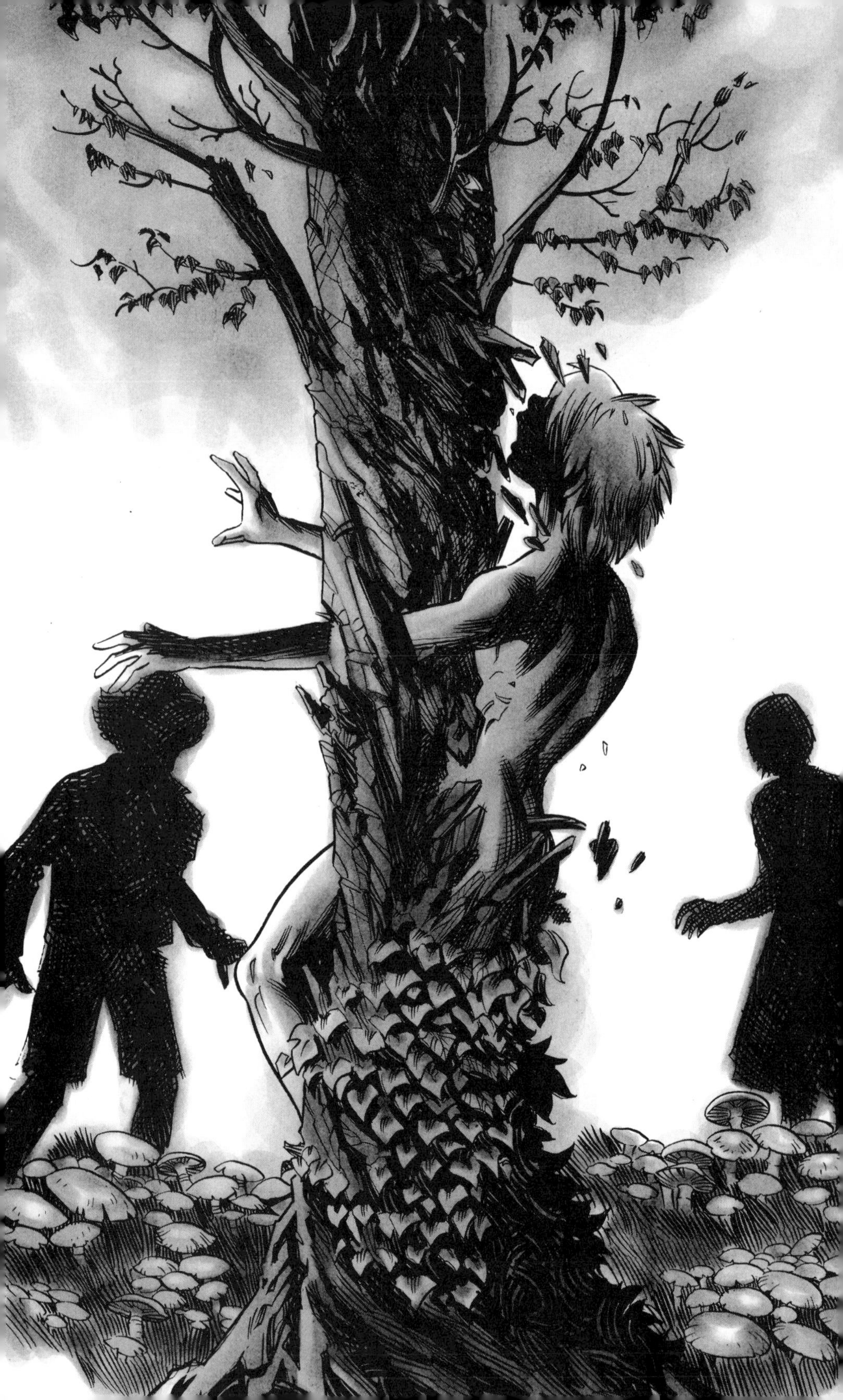

83

84

85

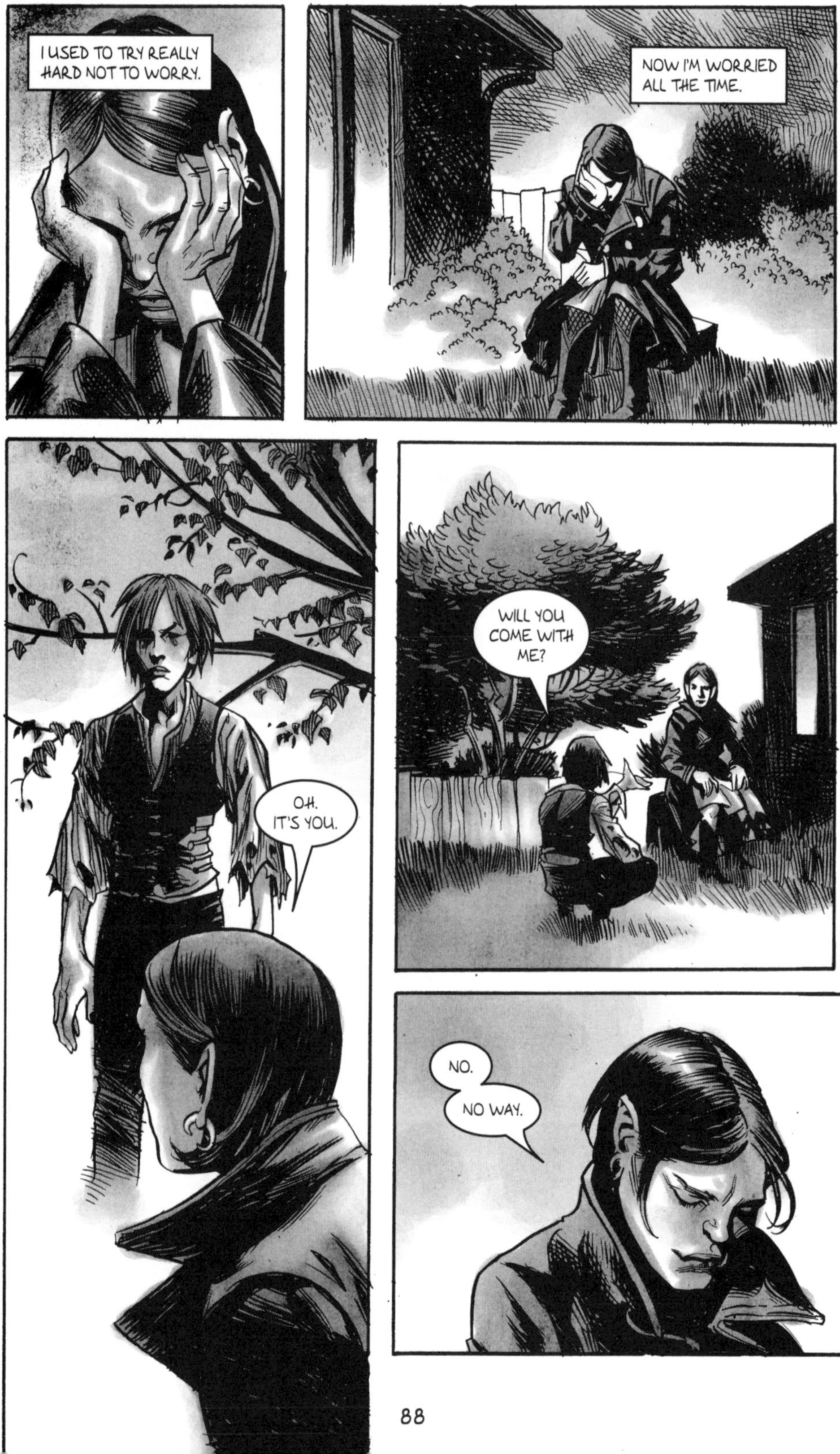
I USED TO TRY REALLY HARD NOT TO WORRY.
NOW I'M WORRIED ALL THE TIME.
OH. IT'S YOU.
WILL YOU COME WITH ME?
NO.
NO WAY.

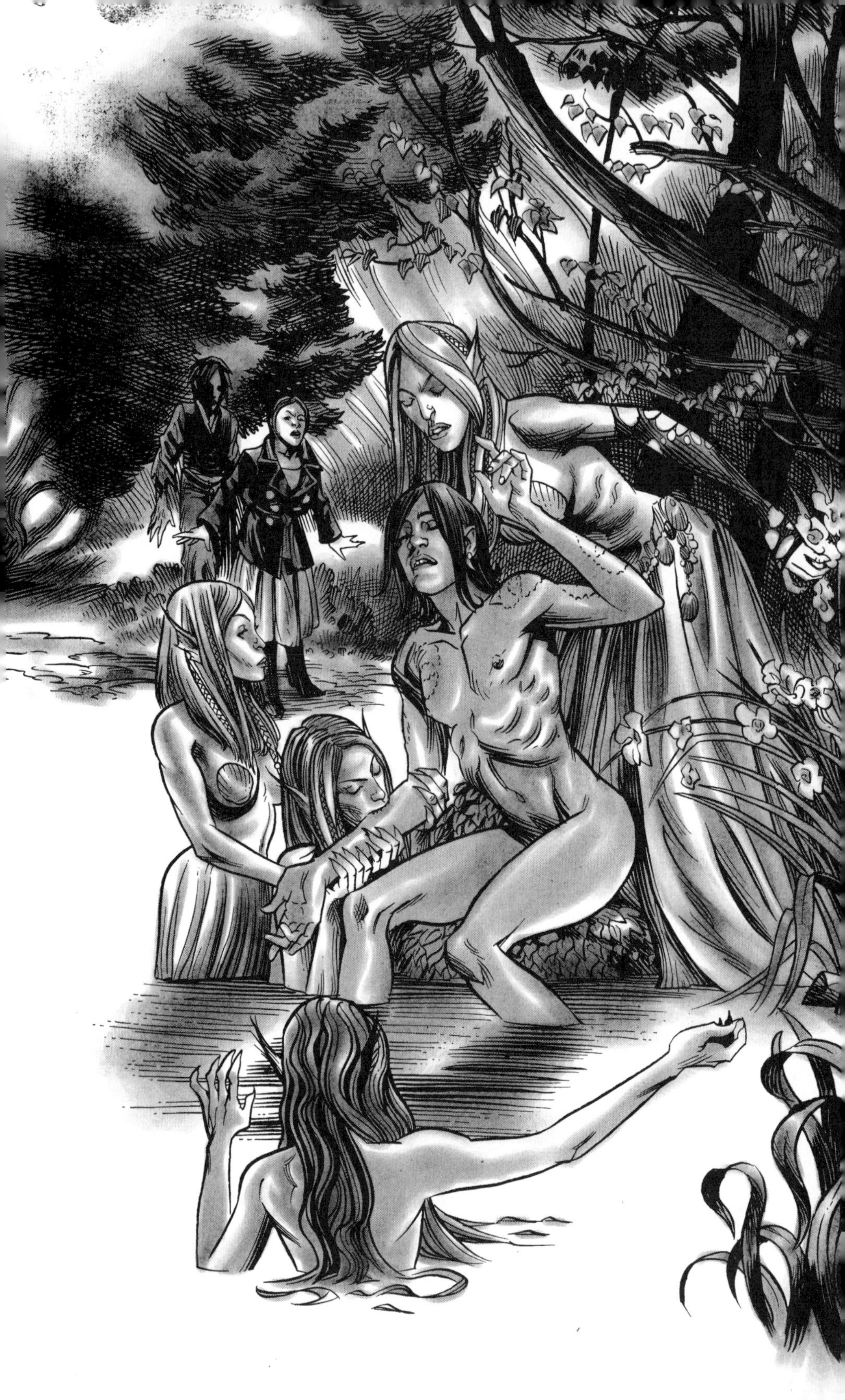

95

91

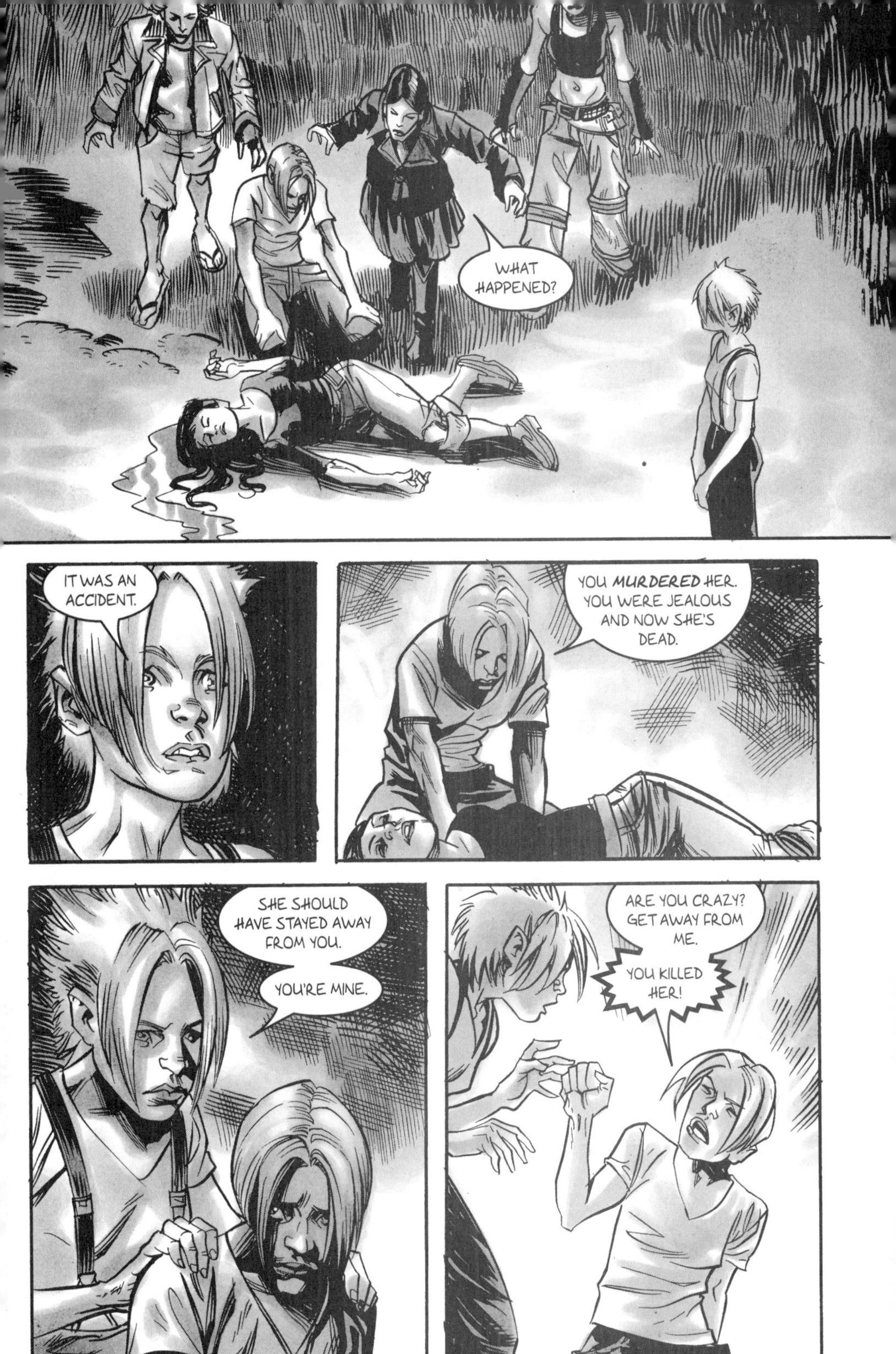
WHAT HAPPENED?
IT WAS AN ACCIDENT.
YOU **MURDERED** HER. YOU WERE JEALOUS AND NOW SHE'S DEAD.
SHE SHOULD HAVE STAYED AWAY FROM YOU.
YOU'RE MINE.
ARE YOU CRAZY? GET AWAY FROM ME.
YOU KILLED HER!

101

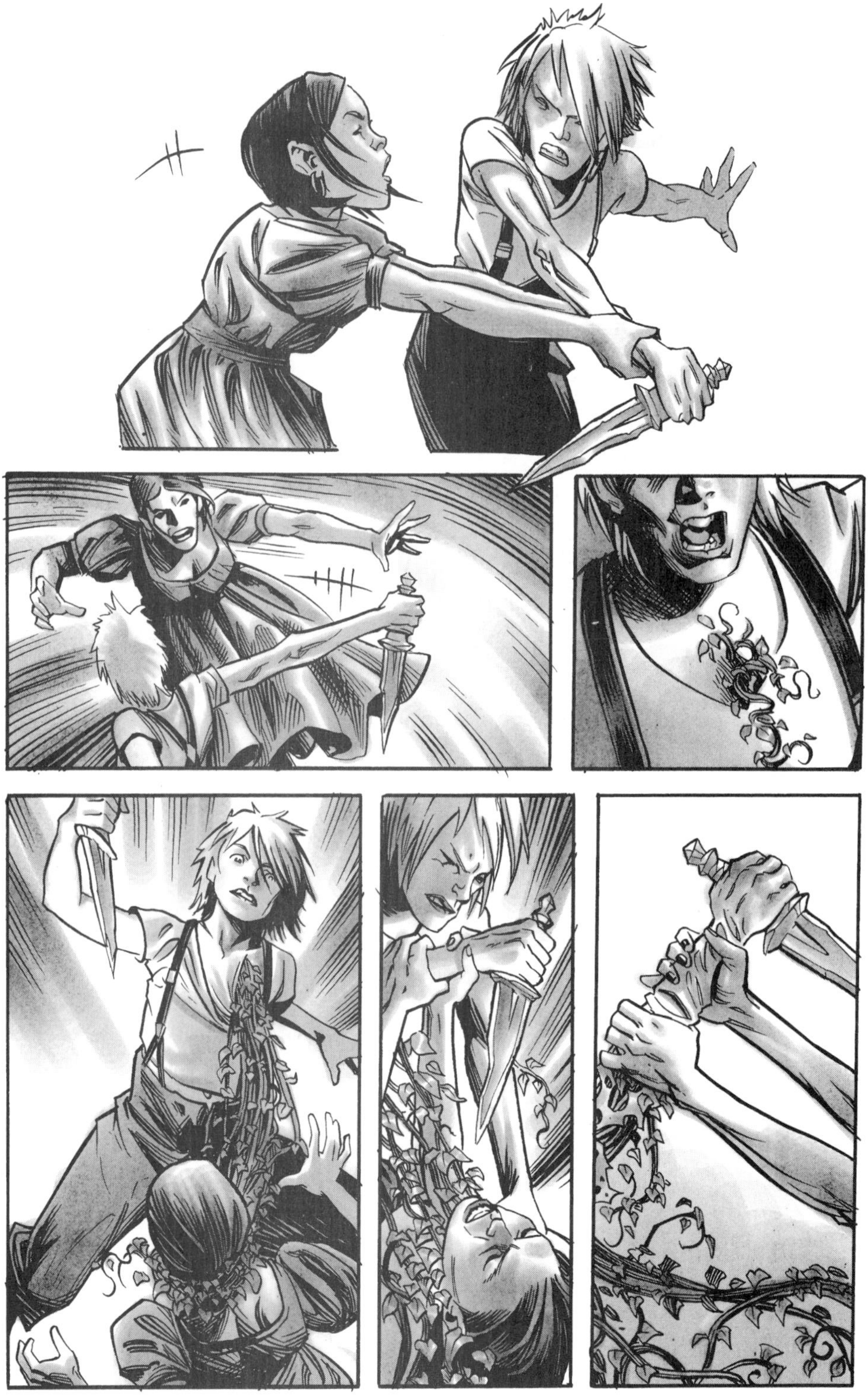

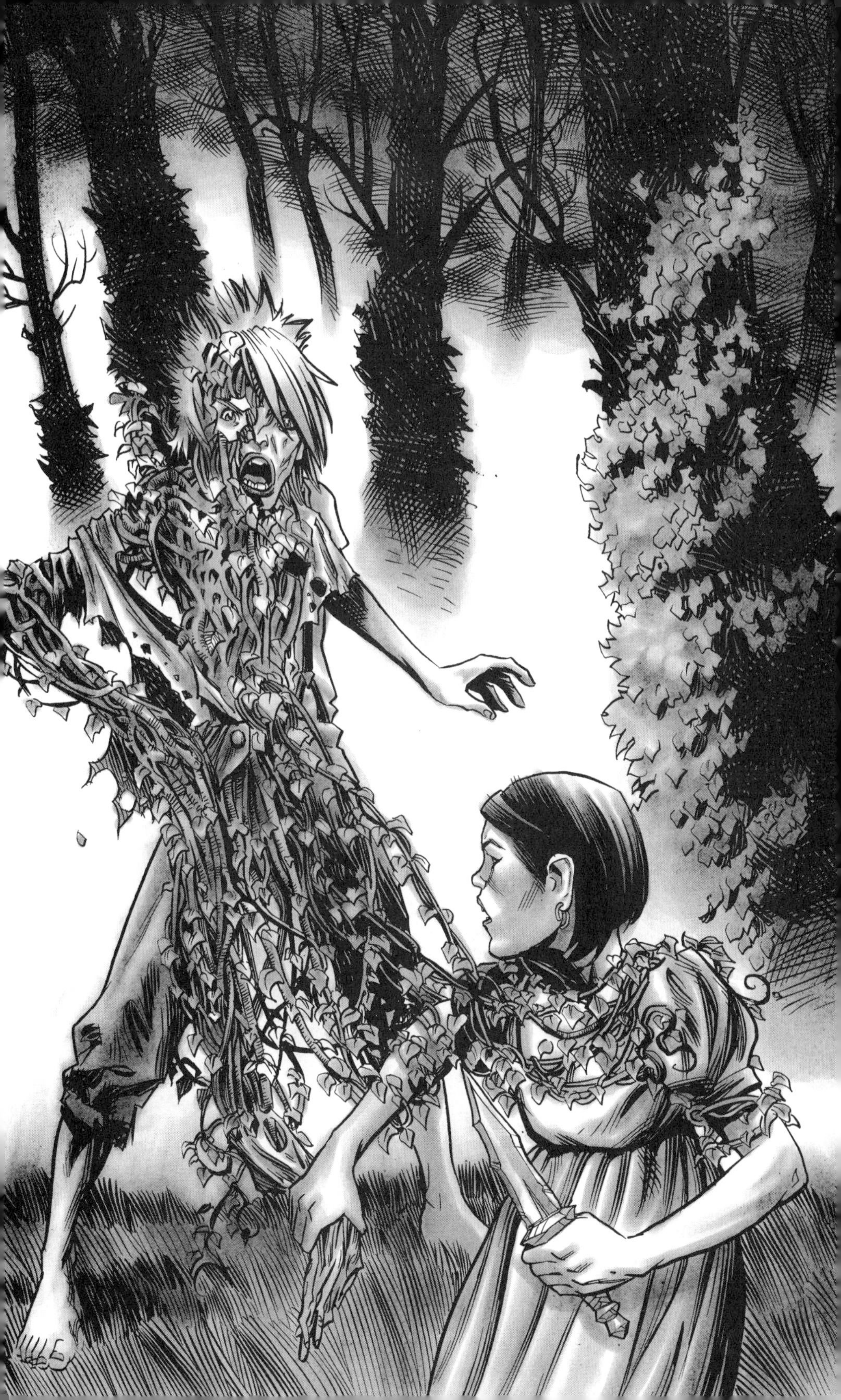

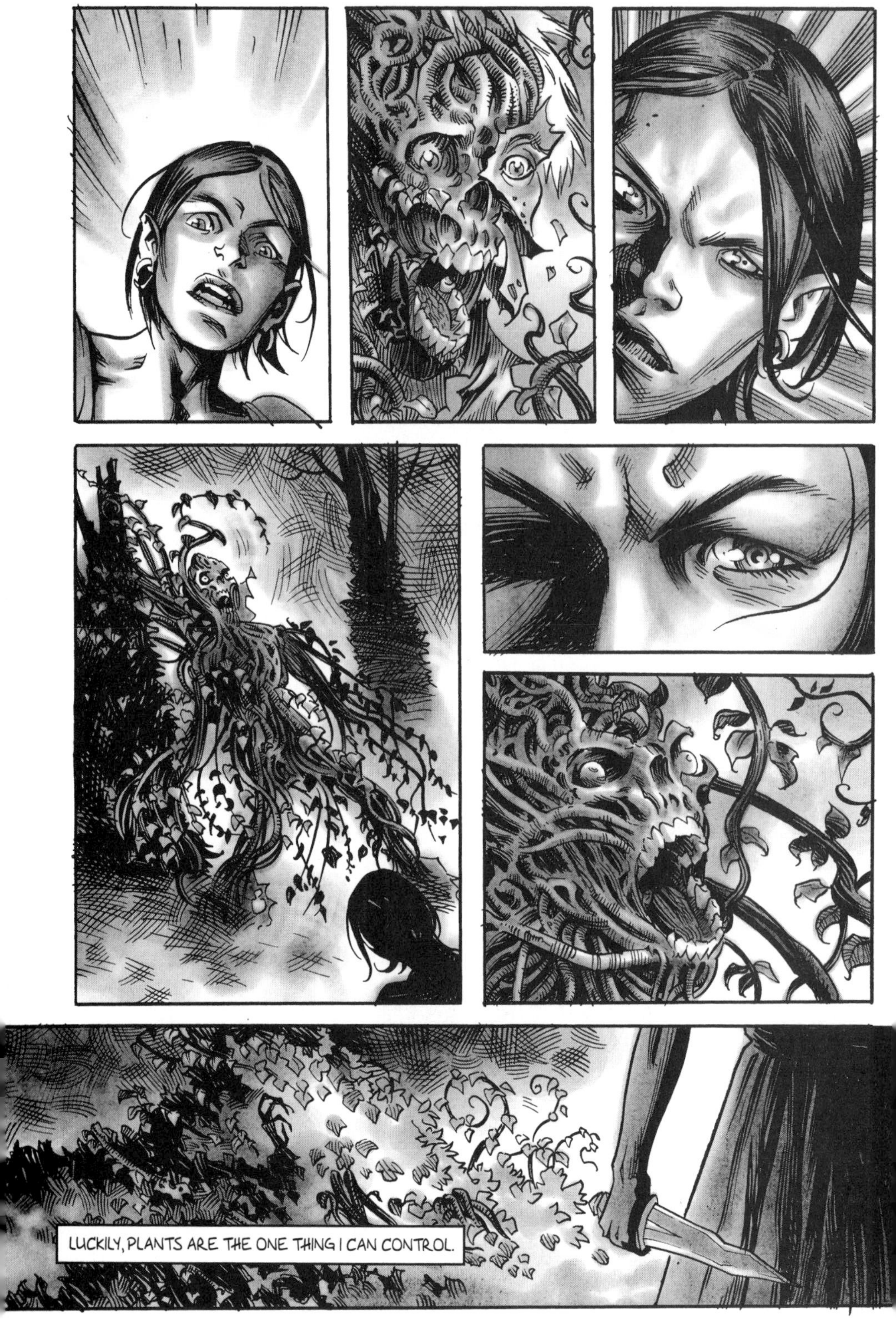
LUCKILY, PLANTS ARE THE ONE THING I CAN CONTROL.

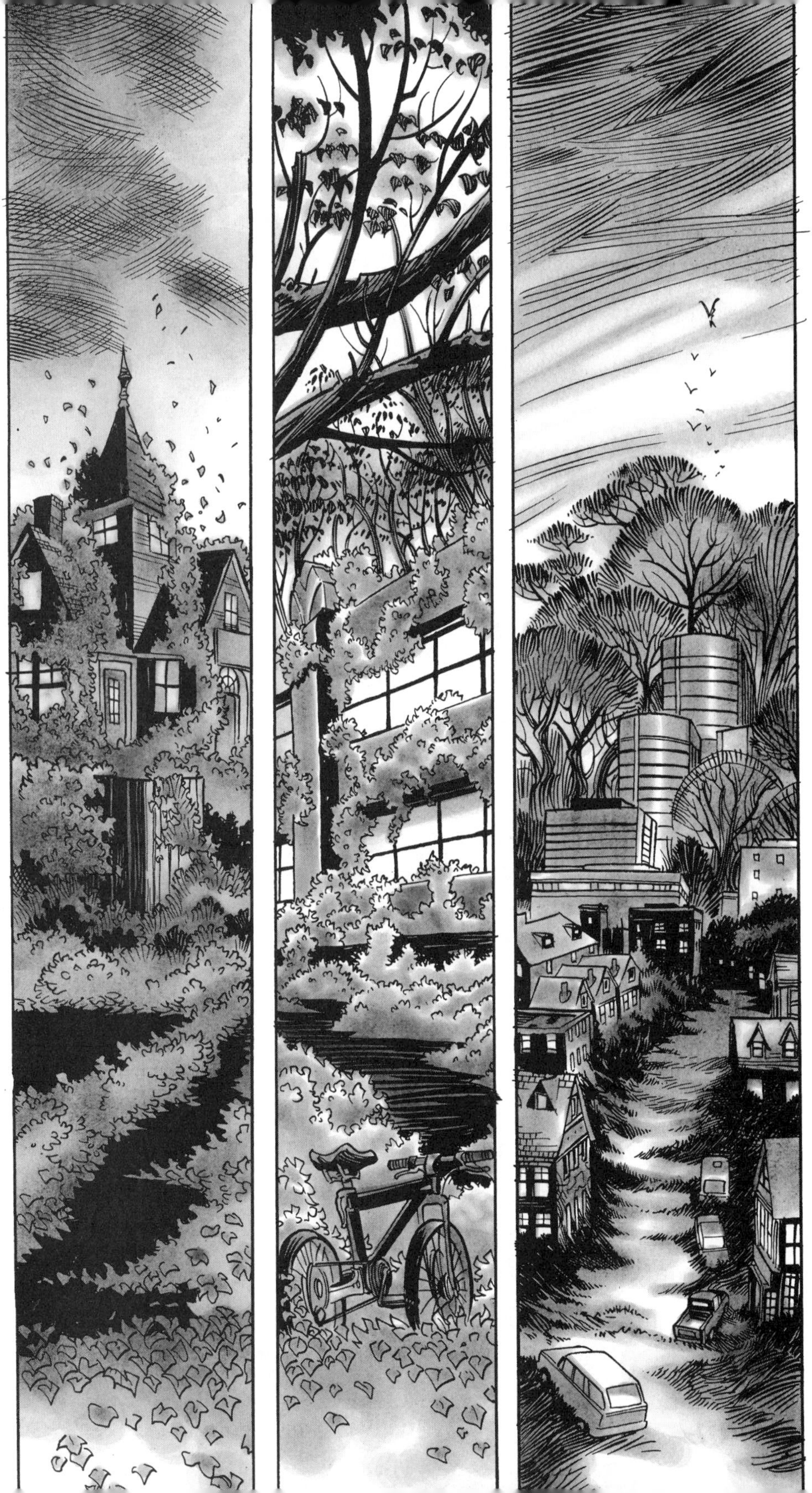

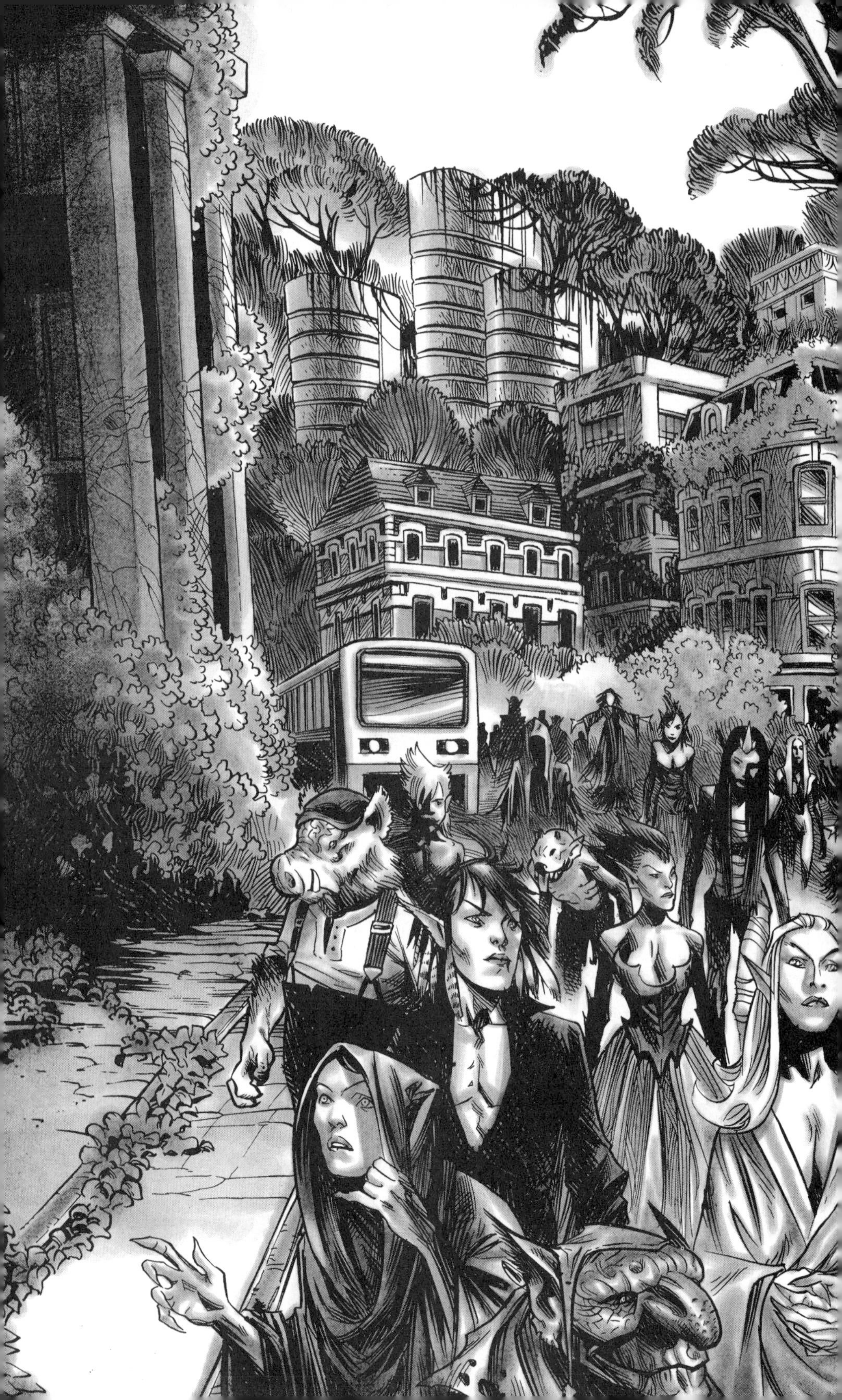

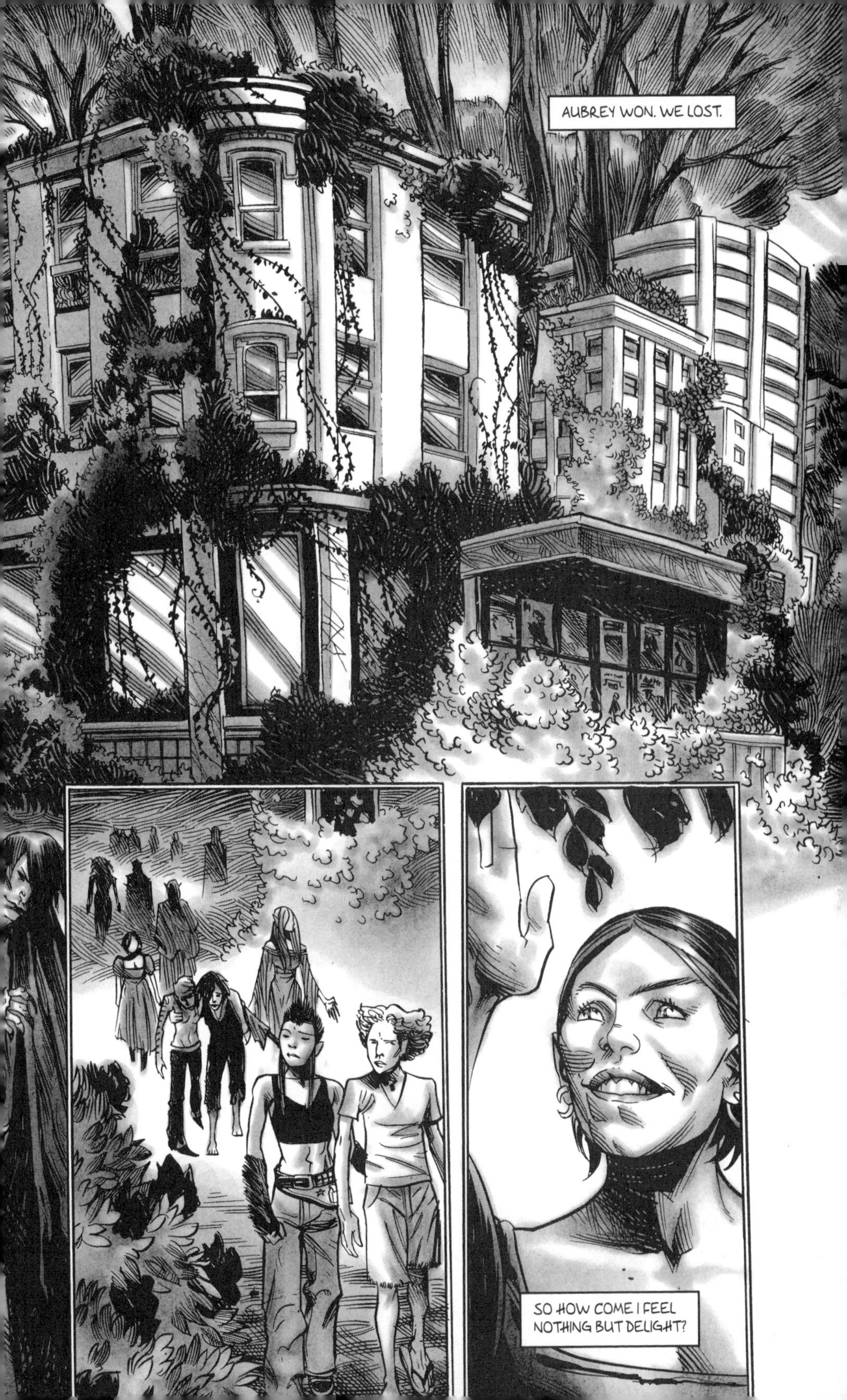
AUBREY WON. WE LOST.
SO HOW COME I FEEL NOTHING BUT DELIGHT?

end of book two

ABOUT THE AUTHOR

Holly Black is the author of contemporary fantasy novels for teens and children. Born in New Jersey, Holly grew up in a decrepit Victorian house piled with books and oddments. She never quite recovered.

Her first book, *Tithe: A Modern Faerie Tale*, was called "dark, edgy, beautifully written and compulsively readable" by *Booklist*, received starred reviews from *Publisher's Weekly* and *Kirkus*, and was included in the American Library Association's Best Books for Young Adults. Holly has since written two other books in the same universe: *Valiant*, a recipient of the Andre Norton Award for Excellence in Young Adult Literature, and *Ironside*.

Holly collaborated with her long-time friend, Caldecott Honor–winning artist Tony DiTerlizzi, to create the best-selling Spiderwick Chronicles. The serial has been called "vintage Victorian fantasy" by the *New York Post*, and *Time* reported that "the books wallow in their dusty Olde Worlde charm." The Spiderwick Chronicles were adapted into a film in 2008.

Holly is currently working on a curse magic caper novel called *The White Cat*.

She lives in Massachusetts with her husband, Theo, and an ever-expanding collection of books. She spends a lot of her time in cafes, glaring at her laptop and drinking endless cups of coffee.

ABOUT THE ARTIST

Ted Naifeh swooped onto the comics and goth culture scene as the co-creator of *Gloomcookie* with Serena Valentino in 1998. Ted illustrated the first volume of the gothic romance hit before departing to pursue his own projects.

In 2002, he introduced us to the world of Courtney Crumrin, a young loner girl who learns magic from her mysterious and curmudgeonly Uncle Aloysius and uses it to navigate her world of school bullies and bloodthirsty goblins, adolescent peer pressure and deadly coven politics. Courtney's adventures have been published in five volumes: *Courtney Crumrin and the Night Things*, *Courtney Crumrin and the Coven of Mystics*, *Courtney Crumrin in the Twilight Kingdom*, *Courtney Crumrin and the Fire-Thief's Tale*, and *Courtney Crumrin and the Prince of Nowhere*.

Ted's next creation was *Polly and the Pirates*, also published through Oni Press, a swashbuckling tale of proper, rule-abiding young Polly Pringle, who is spirited away from her comfortable boarding school existence by pirates who insist that she is their rightful queen and captain. *Polly and the Pirates* was nominated for a Harvey Award.

Ted has also illustrated six volumes featuring video game character Death Jr. for Image Comics, and is the co-creator of *How Loathsome*, strictly for the 18-and-up crowd.

Ted lives in San Francisco, which influenced his aesthetic from a young age with its magnificently spooky Victorian houses, romantic foggy nights, and significant population of Night Things and other fantastic beings.

ACKNOWLEDGMENTS

A lot of people had a hand in pushing me to try writing a graphic novel and helping me along the way. Thanks to Jon Shestack and Ellen Goldsmith-Vein in particular, for asking me about another faery story and liking the one that I told them. Thanks to Steve Burkow for his calm counsel. I am indebted to my literary agent, Barry Goldblatt, and to my editor, the ever-encouraging and amazing David Levithan. And to Ted Naifeh, who brought these characters to life.

I am grateful to Cecil Castellucci, Kelly Link, Justine Larbalestier, Steve Berman, and Cassandra Clare for pushing me to write better and more cleverly. Thanks to Theo for letting me know when things made sense. And thanks to all of you for putting up with my whingeing.

I was greatly inspired by two books, *The Cooper's Wife Is Missing* by Joan Hoff and Marian Yeates and *The Burning of Bridget Cleary* by Angela Bourke. This book was written with the program Scrivener.

– **Holly Black**

I'd like to thank my girlfriend, Kelly, for pestering Cassie Clare into friendship, and Cassie for suggesting me to Holly. Thanks to both Cassie and Holly for not freaking out at us weird San Francisco kids. I'd also like to thank Phil Falco for the gentle, cheerful nudging, and for being a friendly voice getting me out of bed before the day was completely wasted. Sorry it ran so late.

– **Ted Naifeh**